ALIEN ABDUCTION FOR PROFESSIONALS

THE INTERGALACTIC GUIDE TO HUMANS

BOOK 2

SKYE MACKINNON

Peryton Press

Cover by Peryton Covers.

Published by Peryton Press.

skyemackinnon.com

ALIEN ABDUCTION

for professionals

CONTENTS

LESSON 1

TAKING YOUR ABDUCTEE TO A PUBLIC PLACE

TRISH

I patted the wall, stroking it like a pet. "You're a good little ship, Jade," I muttered. "Please don't fail."

The hull groaned in response and the floor beneath me shuddered.

"This can't be normal," I exclaimed, glaring at the guys who'd been telling me that everything was okay.

"No, it's not," Xil sighed. "We should have taken the long way round rather than flying through the nebula. It's too late now. You better put on your seatbelt, it might get even bumpier."

He himself was already strapped into his chair, looking very much like the starship captain he was.

"By A'Ta, what the klat are you doing?" Matar's voice came through the intercom. He was down in the engine room, fixing something – his favourite pastime. To be fair, the Jade constantly needed repairing. She was an old lady who'd seen better days, but she'd been well looked after. The colourful corridors were proof of that, painted by Matar himself. It was the only time I'd ever seen him embarrassed, when I'd told him how much I liked his art. He'd muttered something about randomly throwing paint at the walls and that it was nothing, but I knew how pleased he'd been by my compliments.

"Our captain decided to show off," Havel explained mildly. "Which is why we're now flying through a radioactive nebula instead of taking the scenic route around it."

"I wasn't-" Xil protested but was interrupted by a bang against the hull to my right. I jumped and realised I'd not put my seatbelt on yet. I quickly did so, just in case. I trusted Xil's flying abilities, but this was the first time I'd encountered a nebula and wasn't quite sure what that entailed. Until now, flying through space had mainly consisted of endless darkness with the occasional bright stars glittering in the distance. Not much different from looking up at the night sky on Earth, except that they were much brighter and everything felt more *real*. It was hard to describe the feeling of frightful wonder that overcame me whenever I looked out into the depths of space. Today though, we were going to visit a space station - a treat for me before we were turned into guinea pigs for Professor Katila.

"Get out of there!" Matar shouted. "The engines are overheating, and the radioactive energy is affecting the shields. The Jade is too old for this, you should know that."

"She can do it," Xil insisted. "We're almost through. Don't you want to spend extra time on Kitt-Y-6? This short cut will get us there before lunchtime."

"There might be some pawan steaks left. Trish, you need to try those. They'll fill you up and... never mind."

"What?" I asked.

"Make you horny," Xil chuckled. "Not sure if it's the same for females, but if I eat an entire pawan steak, my cocks will be hard for hours."

"How is that even possible?"

The Jade shook and groaned even worse than before, stopping the guys from answering. I was intrigued, but really, none of us needed aphrodisiacs. I'd lost count of how many times the guys had been inside me, how often I'd sucked them off, how often I'd had them between my legs. I should be sore, but Havel had given me a dose of medical nanites that were helping with any damage both space radiation and too much sex could do to my body.

Space was dangerous, they'd told me that from the start. There wasn't much research on how humans fared if they spent more than a couple of months in space. I supposed that would be an extra bonus for Professor Katila. I was a guinea pig for both her research and her teachings. At least the guys were only used as examples for Katila's lessons.

Again, the ship made noises reminding me of a cry for help. The Jade was suffering. Xil looked conflicted, but he didn't change our course.

"Not much longer," he said soothingly. I wasn't sure if that was meant for the ship or me or him. "Almost through."

I clung to my chair as we swerved and rattled through the nebula. I was starting to feel like I was about to be sick. As much as I appreciated a shortcut to get to the space station a little quicker, I didn't think it was fair on the Jade nor on my stomach.

Kitt-Y-6 was the closest space station to Earth - or Peritus, as the entire galaxy except humans called it -

and my guys had promised me a treat once we got there. I was excited, but also a little trepidatious. I was about to meet a whole lot of aliens. I'd only just got used to my own three aliens and the three-eyed professor who kept checking on us via video link. According to Havel, at least two thousand different species were strewn across the universe. And since not all of the universe had been explored, it was likely that there were many more. The majority of them weren't spacefaring civilisations, so I'd only get to meet around a hundred different kinds of aliens. I snorted. That was still a hell of a lot. Havel, Matar and Xil were all Kardarians, yet they had very different features. Havel was blue and had fangs, Xil sported yellow scales and two cocks (my favourite attribute!) and Matar's green skin was speckled with silver spots that sparkled in bright light. I wasn't sure what wonders would await me at the space station with so much diversity within one species.

"Are there some kind of rules on Kitt-Y-6?" I asked to distract myself from the ominous rumbling the Jade was producing. "To stop people from eating each other?"

Xil laughed. "Yes. All space stations are neutral zones. No eating, no fighting, no blood-sucking, no mating."

"No mating?"

"There have been intergalactic wars brought on by lovesick aliens," Matar explained. "If the wrong species come together to mate, it might even have catastrophic health impacts."

"Not just for the couple," Xil added. "Badengas emit a toxic gas when they climax. It's supposed to protect them from predators during mating, but there was once a case where an entire space station had to be evacuated due to a Badenga having a little too much fun."

I snorted with laughter. "I can see why that would be a problem. I guess we can wait with the mating until we're back on the Jade."

Xil gave me a heated look. "We could always start now..."

The ship lurched to the right and it took all my willpower to prevent my stomach from emptying its contents. No, can't say I was in the mood for sex. As hot as my three males were, puking on them wasn't high on my agenda.

"How much longer?" I winced.

"A half of your Peritus hours," Havel replied. "Which is about twenty IG clicks."

He's explained the intergalactic time system to me before, but I found it very confusing. Since no species wanted to agree on which planet's rotation to use as a day, they averaged the amount of waking and sleeping hours most sentient species need. One IG day was about 27 Earth hours, while ten IG days made up an IG week. I kept getting mixed up with all the numbers, but luckily the guys had done their research and knew how to convert times and dates to what I was used to.

"Aaaaaand we're out of the nebula," Xil announced. Everyone breathed a sigh of relief, me loudest of all. The danger of puking was over.

"You better get changed," Matar told me. "You showing this much skin might be dangerous, even on a station like Kitt-Y-6."

Yes, it probably was a bad idea to go shopping while wearing nothing but my panties and a flimsy bra.

I MET the guys at the airlock. Xil had parked us in the station's spaceport and bought us an electronic parking ticket valid for something like six Earth hours. Enough time to explore. The guys had been making plans for days about what they wanted to show me.

"Ready?" Matar asked me and took my hand.

I nodded. "Let's go shopping."

He slapped his tail on the ground, a gesture that I'd learned is close to him rolling his eyes. All three males didn't seem to think much of shopping, but I'd assured them that it was an essential pastime for Peritan women. I may have accidentally let them believe that it was necessary for us to survive...oops.

"Remember the lesson," Xil told the guys. "We show Trish the best shops and will buy her whatever she looks at for at least thirty Peritan seconds. Some things we can buy in front of her, others we will have to do in secret to surprise her later."

"You know I can hear you, right?"

Xil ignored me. "We do have a budget, so let's avoid the more expensive places. No trip to the exotics market for you, Havel. We can't afford that."

It was kind of sweet how they'd planned this entire trip with the same academic fervour they'd shown during the abduction, probing and mating. I knew they loved me, just like I loved them, and it wasn't all just because we were part of Professor Katila's course.

"Matar, Havel, remember that this excursion won't be filmed for the IGU," Xil reminded them as if he'd read my mind. "We will have to write a detailed report later on, so maybe make some notes. We don't want to disappoint the professor."

His last sentence was dripping with sarcasm. None of us was thrilled with the arrangement, but it had been the only way them pass their Alien Abduction for Beginners course. In return for a 'good' grade, we agreed to act as a case study for Professor Katila's Alien Abduction for Professionals class. The guys were given lessons every week that we then had to put into practice. This, taking me into a public place, was the very first one since we'd signed the contract.

To be fair, the lesson wasn't technically about going shopping. That was just a bonus. No, they were supposed to expose me to other aliens without becoming jealous. They were also told to make sure I felt safe and didn't panic, but I didn't see much chance of that happening. I was buzzing with excitement, and there was no space for fear or worry.

DEPRESSURISING COMPLETE, the

computer announced, and the airlock doors slid open, revealing a massive hangar full of spaceships.

It was big enough for at least four football pitches, maybe more. The ceiling was so high that I couldn't see how far it reached. All around us, the noise of engines, machines and aliens talking in dozens of languages pushed against my ears, making me stumble back. I hadn't expected it to be quite this intense. Even though I was sure those ships ran on a fuel not found on Earth, the air smelled of oil and petrol.

Xil put his hand on the small of my back and gently pushed me forward, out of the Jade and into the chaos of Kitt-Y-6.

Circling around strange-looking space ships, we hurried out of the hangar to a sleek elevator.

"Hop in," Matar said with a grin. He seemed just as excited as me about being on the space station.

As soon as all four of us were inside the spacious cabin, the doors closed and a holographic...thing appeared in the centre. It was clearly alien, but I wasn't sure what gender, age, or even what materials it was made from. It resembled a block of yellow gelatine with several slits all around it that could have been eyes, mouths or something altogether different. It bobbed gently up and down and grew in size every few seconds before constricting again. Breathing? Without that movement, I would have assumed it to be some kind of artificial intelligence, but I instinctively knew it to be sentient. The being looked the same from all sides, so I wasn't sure if I was looking at its front or back. I supposed it didn't matter.

"Shopping platform three," Xil requested, clearly used to this alien's strange appearance.

"Have you completed your immigration forms?" the being replied in English. Well, it probably didn't, but I heard English, so that was all that mattered.

"We have," Xil confirmed and lifted his hand, pressing a button on his wrist communicator.

The gelatine blob vibrated, then turned from yellow into red.

"Invalid forms. You will be taken to a secure location."

I stared at the guys. This sounded bad.

"There's been a mistake," Xil argued, his voice calm and collected. "Check them again. Everything is as it should be."

The blob's expression didn't change - because it didn't have an expression in the first place - but its red faded into a dark orange.

"Full biosignature required. Please press against the walls and stay still until I tell you to move."

This was becoming stranger and stranger. Not how I'd imagined a shopping trip to the space station. It didn't bode well for the rest of our time here.

"Stand against the wall," Xil told me. "It's painless, just a quick scan to confirm that we're the species we say we are."

"How could we pretend to be another species?" I

asked and stepped back until my bum hit the cold elevator wall.

"There are ways. Not that I'm familiar with any of them, of course." Xil gave me a wink.

The elevator began to shake slightly, and I was glad I was pressed against the wall for support. My skin tingled, and a shiver ran down my back.

"Scan complete. Three Kardarians, one human. Interspecies sexual contact confirmed."

"Why do they need to know that?" I whispered, a blush heating my cheeks.

"What is your relationship with these males?" the cube asked me, flashing an alarming red. "Mate, slave, partner, adopted sibling, teacher, student, breeder, nurse, pet-"

"Mate," I interrupted it before it could go any further. "I'm their mate."

It felt good to say that.

The alien stopped flashing and returned to a calming yellow. "Truth verified. Please note that slavery is forbidden on Kitt-Y-6. Should your relationship status change, please notify one of the attendants. Transporting you to shopping platform three. Have a pleasant time."

LESSON 2

SHOPPING FOR RICH(ISH) MALES

MATAR

I slammed my tail against the elevator when we exited. That klatting thing had spoiled the beginning of our excursion. Trish seemed a little downcast, but her expression brightened as soon as she took in our surroundings. It had been a good choice to start with platform three. This was the place where merchants from all across the galaxy came to show off their bestselling wares. The other shopping platforms were more specific, while this was a treasure finder's paradise. There was everything from food to clothing to technology.

"This is amazing," Trish gasped. I had to smile at seeing her so stunned. I remembered my first visit to Kitt-Y-6. It was unlike any other space station. Others were more strict with what could be sold, while here the only rule was no slaves and no weapons. Of course, some merchants would sell you guns and ammunitions if you had the right passwords, but as long as no violence erupted on the station, the officials turned a blind eye.

"What smells so delicious?" our human asked and wrinkled her adorable nose.

"About a hundred different dishes," Havel laughed. "You'll have to be more specific."

"Let's have a wander," I suggested. "When you see or smell something interesting, we'll stop to take a closer look. The only thing we really need is some more clothes for you, but I assume we'll end up with bags full of other stuff."

Xil, Havel and I had listened to a lesson by Professor Katila on shopping with females. It had been an eye-opener. I had no idea females were this obsessed with acquiring new possessions. Katila had given us some pointers on how to resist, but I knew I couldn't resist whenever Trish fluttered her eyelashes and looked at me with a pleading expression that promised I'd be rewarded for giving in. We'd need to stock up on some of her favourite foods and treats, or I wouldn't get to see that lash-fluttering as often. She had a strange taste and liked dishes I wouldn't have touched even if someone paid me to eat them, but after all, she was a different species.

"What's that?" Trish asked and hurried towards a garishly purple stall. "Are those earrings?"

"Translators," the shop owner replied with a charming smile that made me want to punch him. "Not all people want theirs implanted or some kind of ugly device. This is the most fashionable way to show that you're open to other cultures and willing to talk to them."

"That makes no sense," Xil grumbled. "You could easily lose them and then you're stuck without a translator. No, implants are the way to go."

"Look, over there," I said quickly and pointed at another stall. "I think they have piki cakes."

"Pikis!" Havel roared and ran there as if he was starving.

Just like I'd hoped, Trish forgot all about the weird translator jewellery and followed Havel to the food stall. The owner, a massive Intaran female with enough body fat to last her through several famines, wasn't as charming as the other seller. She simply looked at us as if she knew she had no need of charm and sales pitches. Everyone loved piki cakes. I didn't know how it was possible, but almost every species in the galaxy enjoyed these small, moist cakes. The recipe was closely guarded, and I'd never met a piki seller who'd even say if there was meat, plants or something else entirely in them. Not that it mattered.

"Fifty cakes, please," Havel ordered.

The Intaran's expression changed to something more pleasant, while Xil scowled at Havel. Fifty cakes were excessive and would swallow a large part of our budget. Professor Katila had warned us that we'd have to adjust our budget when shopping with a female, but this wasn't Trish ordering an extortionate amount of cakes.

"Where shall I deliver them to?" she asked. "It'll take me a while to wrap them all."

Havel pressed his communicator against the receiver on her table to transmit our parking spot data. "Give us four to go, the rest can be delivered. No need to hurry, we'll be here for a while."

"I assume they're some kind of delicacy?" Trish asked when we walked away from the stall. "You seem to be very keen on them."

Havel laughed. "Wait until you've tried one. You'll never want to eat anything else."

"Which is impossible because we couldn't afford it," Xil muttered, but humour glinted in his eyes. He loved piki cakes just as much as the rest of us.

The medic handed Trish one and she unwrapped it eagerly, revealing the dark red cake. It was stamped with the traditional Intaran symbol that marked it as an original. Many people had tried to replicate them, but none had succeeded.

Trish took a first bite and her eyes widened. "This is amazing. What's it made of?"

"Nobody knows," I explained, "but don't let that stop you. It's not harmful."

She stopped eating. "You don't know? How can you eat something without knowing what it is?"

Havel chuckled. "Do you really care after tasting it?"

Trish took another bite, then shrugged. "Point taken. I'm glad you ordered that many."

We continued walking while enjoying our piki cakes, ignoring the other food stalls for now. We might return to them later, but the cakes would sate us for a while. Despite their small size, they were as filling as a full meal.

"Let's have a look over there," Xil said and led us towards a tech stall. "I could do with some upgrades to my communicator."

I suspected that wasn't what Trish was interested

in, so I took her hand and pulled her the other direction. "You do that while Trish and I will continue to explore. Get me some upgrades too. My holo screen has been flickering recently."

Before the others could protest, we disappeared into the crowd. I was glad to be alone with Trish. Living in such close quarters on the ship, it was hard to spend some time with just her.

"Where are we going?" she asked.

I shrugged. "Wherever you like. Shall we look at clothes?"

Professor Katila had emphasised how important clothing was to females. Especially shoes.

"Yes - wait, what are those?"

She hurried towards a pet stall. Oh no. Xil had told me to avoid those. Larger animals were sold on one of the other shopping platforms, but pets and smaller service animals could also be found on this platform. Klat. Xil would kill me if I allowed her to get a pet. But looking at her expression as she took in the animals whining, barking, chirping and meowing from their cages, I knew that it was too late.

"Welcome, welcome," the owner called from behind a massive aaven who was getting its scales polished. Those six-legged beasts were prized as guard animals, but they were also great with children and would often be the first mount of juveniles living in rural areas. No, we were not getting an aaven.

"What are you in the mood for, my dear? We've just

had a delivery of loovins. They're aquatic, but each comes with a floating liquid-filled bubble so you can take them with you wherever you go. They're long-lived, very loyal and don't make any noise."

He pointed at a stack of glass balls, each housing a strange-looking creature with fins twice as large as their bodies. I had no idea why anyone would want those as a pet. The word pet implied that you could touch and stroke the animal, but I doubted you could do that with loovins.

To my relief, Trish ignored both the aaven and the loovins. Instead, she stared at the tribitts housed in a large cage beneath the stall. I remembered how we'd once mentioned them in conversation. I dimly recalled that Xil even told her she could have one.

The little long-eared creatures were a sorry sight. While the other pets were all in pristine condition, the tribitts looked like they'd not been brushed in days. They were well-nourished but clearly hadn't been given the same attention as the other animals.

"Those are tribitts," the owner said dismissively. "Very old-fashioned. Nobody wants them nowadays. I only keep them because nostalgic tribitt enthusiasts need new breeding females for their herds."

"Ooooooh," Trish exclaimed. "You told me about them, Matar. You didn't say that they look like rabbits!"

"That's because I have no idea what a rabbit is," I chuckled. "But if you say so..."

"What's a rabbit?" the stall owner asked curiously. "Are they cute?"

"Very," Trish replied with a dreamy expression. "I used to have one as a child. They have ears just like these tribitts, but they're a bit smaller and less colourful. Mine was white with beige spots, but you'll also find black and brown ones."

"That sounds dull," I remarked. "It would make them hard to spot."

She laughed. "That's the point. In the wild, they're prey and need to camouflage."

"They're not bred to be pets?" the seller asked with a strange expression. "You take them from the wild?"

He looked horrified at the idea.

"No, but their ancestors were wild. Wait, does that mean tribitts don't exist in nature?"

The stall owner shook his head. "All these pets were created to be just that. Pretty, cute, easy to look after, house or space ship trained. Most of them listen to simple commands, while others are more intelligent. Tribitts can be too clever for some owners, especially when it comes to food. They're known to learn how to open drawers. I've even heard of some that can manipulate a fabricator. That could be just a myth, but I wouldn't put it past them. Devious little beasts. I don't know why they were even created. Now, my dear, how about one of these gorgeous Sliviean poro'la? They like to ride on their owner's shoulder and are excellent at removing body hair."

One look at Trish told me that we'd leave Kitt-Y-6 with a tribitt. And when she looked at me and began to flutter her lush eyelashes, I knew I had no choice.

"Which one do you like best?" I asked, repressing a sigh.

Most of the tribitts in the cage were a shade of dark purple with bright pink ears. Two were golden with dark stripes, and-

"The green one," Trish said determinedly. "It's the same shade as you. So pretty."

My heart did a little jump at that. She chose that tribitt because it reminded her of me. I would have bought her a dozen tribitts just to hear her say that again.

"Are you sure?" the owner asked, clearly not happy about it. I guessed the other pets were more expensive than the tribitts. After he'd told us that they were out of fashion, he couldn't charge a lot for them, not without losing face. That suited me just fine. We'd have more left in our budget to buy Trish other things. I wanted to treat her to a necklace I'd seen the last time we'd been on Kitt-Y-6. It was unlikely it was still available, but it would suit her perfectly.

"Yes," Trish replied without hesitation. "That is if you're okay with that?"

She turned to me.

"Of course," I said quickly. "Anything for you."

Trish smiled. "I'll give you a proper thank you later."

My cock hardened. I knew exactly what she had in mind.

I squeezed her hand, a promise of other squeezing I was planning on doing later. Her breasts were made for

me, perfectly fitting into my hands. I loved massaging them, using just the right amount of pressure to make her moan and gasp.

"Do you need a basic tribitt accessories set with that?" the stall owner asked, clearly hoping to increase his profits. "It includes a harness, leash, food bowls, litter tray, some toys and a first-aid kit."

"First-aid?" Trish asked with wide eyes. "Do they get injured easily?"

The male grinned. "No, that's for the owners. Tribitts can be moody."

I rolled my eyes. "Don't listen to him. If you treat a tribitt right, he'll never scratch or bite you. But we'll take the set. I assume they're vaccinated and microchipped?"

"Yes, they also have sensors implanted, so you always know where your tribitt is and how it's feeling. There's an app for your communicator."

An app to monitor your tribitt. How silly.

He opened the cage and grabbed the green tribitt by its ears. It let out an angry bellow, but the seller didn't seem to care. I was starting to regret buying from him, but it was too late. The way Trish looked at the tribitt meant she'd already fallen in love with it. Not that I could blame her. The little animal was adorable. While most of it was green, it had small pink spots beneath its eyes. Its paws were a lighter green, the same as the insides of its long ears. Trish had been right. It was almost the exact colour I was.

"Do you want a cage for it?" the seller asked. "Or I can put the harness on it and you can carry it around with you. I should warn you, though, they go crazy for piki cakes so don't let them anywhere near that stall."

I sighed. That was going to be a problem.

LESSON 3

THE INTRICACIES OF MATING TOYS

XIL

I tried to be as quick as possible with getting my essential purchases done. I'd give Matar a good talking-to later for stealing away Trish. That klatting male was going to spend tonight alone in his bedroom, without our human.

While we squeezed through the crowd, Havel played around with the gadget he'd just bought. It was a ring that changed colour depending on Havel's mood. I didn't know why he needed it. Our healer was one of the easiest to read males I'd ever met. Maybe he'd got it for Trish, but since Kardarians and humans were so similar in looks and behaviours, it was really unnecessary. Oh well, it was his money. The IGU paid us for being their case study subjects in addition to giving us the chance of another certification, so we had some money to spare.

"I want to get her a present," Havel suddenly said. "Any ideas?"

I'd had the same idea, and it irked me that he'd said it first. Now he would think that I was copying him.

"Maybe we should ask one of the assistants," I suggested, unwilling to tell him what I'd planned to get Trish. "They might be able to recommend something."

Havel nodded and flagged down one of the AI globes swirling above our heads. Years ago, they used to have real people do this, but they switched to AIs for a 'better service'. To save costs, more like.

"How can I be of assistance?" the AI asked in a seductive female voice. Did they all talk like that or had the AI determined that we'd react best to this voice?

"We want to get our human female a present," I told the flashing globe. "Do you have any suggestions?"

"Data on humans is lacking," the AI replied, managing to sound almost regretful. "Switching to generic female profiles. Does the female like cooking?"

"No," both Havel and I said as one.

"Does she like fashion?"

"We want a present that's something special," I said before it could ask any more stupid questions. "Something that isn't a commodity. Something pretty and valuable. Something that shows her that we love her."

I regretted saying that last bit. Admitting my love for Trish to an AI felt weird.

"Maybe a present that her and I could use together," Havel suggested.

Again, I hated him for coming up with that.

"I know just the thing," the AI chirped. "Follow me."

It led us through the crowd, occasionally hovering above a stall as if it was deciding whether to stop there or not, before continuing. We were halfway through the shopping platform before it finally landed on the roof of a busy stall. Males of all species, sizes and colours were standing around it, staring at the wares on offer. I exchanged a look with Havel. This was a good sign. Those males were likely buying presents for their females, too.

Instead of waiting, I squeezed through the shoppers until I was pressed against the table. A strange selection of objects was spread out in front of me. I had no idea what any of them were, although some of the long objects' shapes reminded me of something. No, that couldn't be... could it?

"Welcome," a shop assistant in barely any clothes greeted us. She was showing more skin than I liked. In the past, before we abducted Trish, I may have found the female attractive, but now I just found it irritating.

"Are you looking for a toy to use with a male, female or other?"

"Toy?" Havel asked.

"Mating toys," the Ferven said, rolling her eyes.

Havel and I looked at each other again. Neither of us knew what this was about.

"Sometimes, you might want to add some more spice to your mating," the female explained with an exasperated sigh. "In the beginning, it's all exciting and new, but at some point, you'll run out of techniques and experiences to try. That's when our famous mating toys come into play. We've got toys for all species and preferences. Kardarians are one-cock-species, correct? Maybe your female would like to experience what it would feel like to be with a two or even three-cock-male? We've got some beautiful replicas, either standalone or as a strap-on."

I wanted to rub my eyes in astonishment. Fake cocks? What was the galaxy coming to? Next, they'd come up with fake pussies and fake boobs.

"Some of us do have two cocks, actually," I told her and flicked my gaze downwards for a second to make it very sure that I was one of those males.

"Apologies," she muttered, but I ignored her and let my gaze wander over the stall's offerings. And instantly corrected my view of the universe when I realised both fake boobs and pussies were available. Including the rubbery replica of a four-boobed Ankanis female. How peculiar. Why would anyone prefer to play with this instead of the real thing? I supposed there were lonely males out there with no chance of ever abducting their own female. Havel, Matar and I were lucky to have found Trish, the most perfect female in the entire galaxy.

"Our female has four Kardarian cocks to choose from," Havel said drily. "What else do you have?"

"Take a look at these magic balls," the Ferven said and held up a chain of three fist-sized balls made of some kind of rubbery material. "They vibrate, and the deluxe version can even emit mating hormones, depending on the species. Or maybe you'd like your female to experience the pleasures of knotting?" She pointed at a strange ring. "Just push this over your cock and at the end of your mating, it will activate, locking you inside your female. You can set the time yourself or you can have it choose a random time. It can be most satisfying to be inside your female for hours, without neither of you able to break the link."

My cock hardened at the thought of being bound to Trish in that way.

"I'll take one," I said before Havel had the chance.

"Would you like small, medium or large?" she asked and held up three different sizes. As much as it pained me to admit, the large one was about three times the girth of my cock. I had no idea what species that was made for, but it had to be some kind of giant.

"Medium," I admitted grudgingly.

She grabbed a box from under the table and handed it to me. I pressed my communicator against the receiver, and it automatically took the credits from my bank account. I'd not even checked how much this knotting ring cost. That was so unlike me. Being with Trish was changing me in all sorts of ways.

"What can I get for you?" the Ferven asked Havel. "How about this little remote-controlled vibe?"

"What's a vibe?"

"Really, don't Kardarians know anything?" she huffed, before putting on a fake smile again. "It's a vibrator. She'll insert it and it will vibrate when you want it to, stimulating her from within. Of course, you can also give her control over it, but most males prefer to be the ones to do the honours. Again, vibes come in all shapes and sizes. What species is your female?"

Havel didn't reply and turned to me instead. "I might just get her some more piki cakes. This is so strange. Who says she even likes these toys? She might be offended if we give them to her."

I gulped. I hadn't thought of that. Hopefully, she didn't mind. Trish loved mating, so she'd also love this, right?

Without another word, Havel walked away from the stall. I grabbed my box and followed him, now very much doubting my purchase. I was going to have to talk to Professor Katila. Her advice about shopping for our female had been completely useless so far.

TRISH

The little tribitt purred in my arms, looking up at me with his beautiful black eyes. There was a certain intelligence to his gaze. I couldn't wait to be back on the ship to play with him. Matar had promised to download a guide to tribitt husbandry to the reading device the guys had borrowed me. The animal looked a bit like a rabbit if you ignored the tiny antennae sprouting between its ears and the colour of its fur, so maybe he had a similar temperament and needs. The seller had reassured Matar that the tribitt was litter trained and wouldn't soil the ship. We'd see if that was true. After seeing how that guy had kept the poor little tribitts, ignoring them in favour of fancy pets that were in fashion, I didn't trust his words.

One of his ears stroked my chin and I laughed. "Aren't you the cutest little bunny," I cooed.

"Tribitt," Matar corrected. "Have you thought of a name yet?"

"No, but I think I'll discuss that with all of you later.

If this is going to be our family pet, we should all have a say."

"Family pet?" he repeated slowly. "I like the sound of that. Family."

I would have hugged him if I didn't have a snuggle tribitt in my arms. I didn't want to squeeze him to death between Matar and me, but I made a mental note to give him that hug later. Maybe paired with a kiss.

"What now?" I asked.

"Are you hungry?"

"Nope, not in the slightest. That cake has made me so full that I don't think I need any food for the next week or so."

He laughed. "And I bet you'll want another piki cake then?"

"You know me so well." I grinned at him. "Is there anything you'd like to buy?"

"Giving you that tribitt has been enough. I don't need anything for myself."

"It's not about needing something. Shopping is all about treating yourself to something you want rather than need."

"Yes, I think I remember Professor Katila saying that. But what if all I want is to spoil my little human mate?"

Warmth spread through my chest and it had nothing to do with the furry animal pressed against me.

"Then maybe I should spoil you... if I had any money."

I sighed. "Not having a job and my own money sucks. I hate relying on you for everything. I don't get why the IGU won't pay me like it does you. I'm part of the case study, aren't I? I should be reimbursed for my troubles, too."

"You're right. As much as I love to care for everything you may desire, I understand the desire to be independent. Maybe we should all give you a share of our pay. That way, it's like a salary from the IGU, even if they don't pay you themselves."

I frowned. "I suppose that would be a good solution. And next time we speak to Professor Katila, I might demand that she pay me if she wants me to co-operate."

"I wouldn't suggest that," Matar said with a sigh. "I've heard stories of her being quite nasty to people who didn't follow her rules. Everyone thinks she's kind and benign because she's a Karangi, but there's something cold behind those three pretty eyes."

"Well, if you're going to pay me my salary, that means I can buy you something now." I smiled. "And I know just the thing."

"Trish!" a familiar voice called from behind me.

I swirled around to see Xil and Havel make their way through the busy crowd. A group of very tall aliens that reminded me of humanoid giraffes stood in their way, but when Xil glared at them, they hastily stepped aside.

They didn't see the little tribitt until they finally reached us, which explained the shocked looks on their faces.

"A pet?" Havel asked before his surprised expression turned into one of adoration. "It's soooo cute! Can I hold it?"

"It's a male," I grinned and handed the green bunny to Havel.

"You've adopted another male?" Xil growled. "Aren't three enough for you?"

I stared at him, but then his scowl cracked and a wide smile appeared on his face.

"Just messing with you. He's adorable. I wondered if you'd buy one after we'd talked about it a while back. I wasn't sure if you'd remember."

"I couldn't resist." I watched as Havel petted the tribitt, rubbing it between its ears. The furry creature purred and sighed in contentment. Awwww. So cute. I was dying of cuteness.

"Does he have a name?" Havel asked, repeating Matar's earlier question.

"No, let's do that later. What did you guys buy?"

Xil didn't meet my eyes. "I'll show you back on the Jade. Let's not do it in public."

"Yeah, let's not," Havel chuckled. "But I can show you mine."

He handed the tribitt to Xil, who immediately grinned goofily and started muttering to the animal. The tribitt seemed to be enchanting everyone. I had no idea why they'd gone out of fashion. I couldn't imagine a cuter pet.

"Hold out your hand," Havel asked and rummaged in his pockets.

Curiously, I did as he'd asked. Had he bought some kind of bracelet for me? Or a ring? Was he going to-

He pulled out a wrist communicator, similar to the ones he and the other guys wore, but smaller and on a leather armband rather than metal. Small pearls had been woven into the material, turning it into jewellery. He slid it over my wrist and fastened it.

"We can set it up on the ship, but I thought it was time for you to have one. You'll be able to control everything on the Jade, communicate with us and whoever else you want, watch those Periton videos you like, use it to-"

I hugged him tightly, pressing a kiss on his cheek. "It's perfect. Thank you."

He wrapped his arms around me and pressed me tight against his chest. I breathed in his scent and wished we were on the Jade already. I needed to thank him and Matar for their gifts, plus I was curious about what Xil had got for me. It had to be something naughty if he couldn't show it in public.

"Maybe I give you mine now so I can get a hug, too," Xil grumbled from behind me.

I laughed and took the tribitt from him. "Later. I promise. What else is on our shopping list?"

My new little pet yawned and wiggled its head into my armpit. Its ears were flat against its head and its eyes slowly fluttered close. Despite the noise around us, it had fallen asleep. No idea how it did that, but I guessed he was used to being surrounded by noise and people. He might even get scared on the Jade where it was a lot quieter, with only the hum of the engines and our voices. Sometimes music, too, but I didn't care much for the Kardarian rock the guys loved so much, and I hadn't been able to convince them of listening to Earth music, either.

"Clothes for you," Xil said. "And we should get some parts for the ship. Matar, that's your job. Didn't you say you needed some kind of special bolts?"

"I did," Matar replied grudgingly, clearly not happy about it. "But can't we get them together after we've been clothes shopping?"

"You've already had alone time with Trish," Havel snarled. I looked at him in surprise. Why was he so angry?

Xil put a large hand on my shoulder and steered me away from Matar and Havel. "Let's get you some clothes. I saw this Ferven female earlier with a very fabric-less outfit. It reminded me of that lingerie you told us about."

I laughed when I remembered how they'd tried to make their own lingerie once. In a misguided attempt to seduce me, they'd cut holes in their clothing. I still didn't know how they could have been that stupid, but I believed it was due to the ridiculous lessons the Intergalactic University had taught them. A lot of what they knew about humans was wrong. Very wrong. Hell, they didn't even get the name of our planet right. They called it Peritus, although apparently it had been given that name long before the first life had developed on

Earth. Still, it felt weird to call good old Earth by another name.

"Shall we get you some?" Xil asked eagerly.

I shook my head but stopped immediately when the tribitt started mewing in his sleep.

"I think I could do with some proper clothes. You know, jeans, shirts, jumpers, maybe even some bras. But nothing too fancy." It's not like we were meeting a lot of other people. I grinned at the thought of other spaceships docking with the Jade in space so we could have a cup of tea with random aliens.

While the guys had some friends outside of their trio, most of them were back on their planet, just like their family. One day, we were going to travel to Kardar so I could meet their parents, but not yet. Kardar was far from Earth - Peritus - and we had better things to do. That's what Xil said, anyway. He hated his father, but I didn't know why. He'd only mentioned his mother once or twice, and I hadn't wanted to pry. He'd tell me at some point, I knew that. We had no secrets from each other, but some things didn't have to be discussed.

The guys led me to a row of clothes stalls. I gaped at the garments. Of course, I should have known that I wouldn't find any Earth clothes here, but it was still a shock to see how different everything was. A shirt to my left had four armholes and it shimmered in all colours of the rainbows even though I could swear that it was white. Something that looked like a hoodie for a two-headed species had an inbuilt screen, showing text in an alien language on its front. Advertising, a political message, quotes from a song? I couldn't read it.

Xil flagged down a little AI globe - I'd seen other aliens use them - and asked it to lead us to a shop catering to humans. The ball whizzed away and we hurried to follow it through the narrowing walkways until we got to a rather sorry looking area. Barely any shoppers, dusty stalls, depressed sellers. Not exactly what I'd hoped for.

"Maybe we should go back," Havel suggested. "This looks seedy."

"Stall 429Y has the best clothes for humanoids," the AI chirped, sounding almost offended. "Please take a look."

It stopped above a lacklustre shop that had clearly seen better days. While other stalls used flashing lights, signs, garish colours and sexy shop assistants to lure in the crowds, this one had nothing but a tired looking alien with one large eye and no nose. The rest of him looked somewhat human in the sense that he only had two arms and two legs, without tentacles, tails or talons. After seeing dozens of different alien species today, I'd gained a new perspective on what was possible.

Xil pointed at a dark green blouse. "This would suit you. Plus, it matches the tribitt."

"And me," Matar grinned. "I love seeing you in my colour."

"You should also get something in yellow and blue then," Havel insisted immediately. "No favouritism."

"We don't stock yellow," the shop owner said in a

monotonous, tired voice. "But we do have various blue shades. How about this skirt?"

He rummaged in a stack of barely folded clothing and pulled out a monstrosity of a skirt. It looked like a dishevelled chicken and a blueberry had a baby. And then added lots of frills. It was so ugly that it could probably count as fashion somewhere in the galaxy.

"No, thanks," I muttered. "Do you have any jeans?"

"Jeans?" he asked, clearly not recognising the word. Maybe my translator didn't know that.

I sighed. "Trousers, thick cloth, hard to destroy. Usually blue. Do you have anything like that?"

"Wouldn't you prefer something more flattering?" the alien insisted and held up a see-through blouse that would have barely covered my boobs.

"It would suit you," Havel whispered from behind me. I elbowed him in the stomach, and he groaned. "Alright, go with something else instead. But it would still look great on you."

I sighed. "Is there somewhere I could try on some of these?"

The cyclops nodded towards his right. "There's a changing pod over there."

I handed the tribitt to Matar and randomly grabbed a couple of items, not convinced I'd like any of them. Still, I didn't want to disappoint the guys by being too choosy. After all, we'd walked for ages to get to this stall and I didn't want to stay in this seedy area any longer than I had to.

The changing pod looked a bit like a port-a-loo, just

more space-y. A silver door slid open when I approached, revealing a small room with mirrored walls. As soon as I stepped inside, the door closed. A light above me flickered into life, but even so, I felt a little claustrophobic without a window. Yup, just like a port-a-loo.

I quickly undressed and tried on the first shirt. It wasn't too bad, although it wasn't flattering in the slightest. I'd take it anyway, just to have something to show for. This shopping trip wouldn't be for nothing. The two pairs of trousers both didn't fit, although I might be able to wear the looser ones with a belt. I should check the stall if they had any. The puke-coloured jumper I'd grabbed was surprisingly comfortable. It looked horrendous, but it was warm and soft. The Jade was usually warm enough to walk around in t-shirts, but who knew when we might visit a colder planet. Better to be prepared.

The final item was a tank top that I wouldn't have chosen if I'd had given it a proper look. It ended above my navel and together with its extremely low cleavage, it didn't leave much to the imagination. The fabric's feel reminded me of neoprene except that it was thinner. My nipples poked through the fabric. Definitely not something I'd wear in public, and if the guys saw me wearing it, I wouldn't keep it on for long. They'd rip it off my body before ravishing me where I stood. Yes, I was speaking from experience.

Suddenly, the pod shook, and I stumbled back against the wall. The cabin swayed, leaning to one side as if someone was trying to push it over from outside.

"Hey, I'm in here!" I shouted as loud as I could. "Stop that!"

Nobody replied, but the movement continued. I dropped to my knees, feeling safer close to the floor. A lurch made me gasp. The pod was being pulled into the air. Fuck. What the bloody hell was happening here?

"Stop!" I cried. "Help!"

It was useless. The pod swayed as if it was swinging in the air. Were they transporting it somewhere else? This couldn't be happening. How did a shopping trip turn into this? All I could hope for was that this was an honest mistake and not an abduction. I doubted I'd ever come across abductors as friendly and cute as mine again.

Fuck. I continued shouting, but nobody heard me. Or if they did, they didn't care.

With nothing else to do, I put on my own clothes again, then wrapped my arms around my knees and hoped that my guys would find me soon.

LESSON 4

INTRODUCTION TO RESCUING YOUR FEMALE

"Shouldn't she be back by now?" I asked, checking the time. "It's been ages."

"Females can take a while when trying on clothes," the Brontes said, looking unconcerned.

We declined. If his *refreshments* were the same quality as his stall, we'd likely end up with food poisoning.

"Maybe ping her communicator," Xil suggested. "Just to check if she needs help deciding."

My present for her was already coming in handy. I'd made the right choice, even though it had taken me forever to decide.

I dialled her communicator's ID and waited for her to respond. I hadn't shown her how to use it yet, but all she had to do to pick up a call was press one very obvious button or use voice control. I'd made sure the device had human English installed as a language.

"The changing rooms are data-insulated," the Brontes told me. Was that a smirk on his thick lips? "We don't want customers to be disturbed while trying on clothes. It's an intimate process, after all."

That didn't make sense to me, but I didn't know much about fashion. I bought my clothes in bulk and put on whatever was on top of the stack in my wardrobe. Now that we were part of Professor Katila's case study, we had to wear slightly more formal clothes, but Trish had assured me that my black garments would be fine.

We waited for a little while longer until I couldn't stand it any longer.

"I'm going to check on her," I announced and headed off to where we'd last seen Trish. She'd disappeared behind the stall, but when I scanned the dirty, rubbish-strewn area at the back of the shops, there was no changing pod. Strange. A few doors led away from the main shopping area into the belly of the space station, but those were out of bounds and likely locked. She wouldn't have gone into one of them. So where was Trish?

I called out to the others, but they were already close behind me.

"Where is she?" Matar asked and sniffed the air. "I can smell her scent, she's been here, but where did she disappear to?"

"Let's ask that Brontes," Xil growled. "He can lead us to that mysterious changing pod."

A strangely muffled cry made me look up just in time to see a silver pod disappear through a hatch in the ceiling.

Someone had taken Trish.

I exchanged a look with the guys and without another word, we broke into a run.

It took us way too long to reach the nearest elevator. It took even longer for the warden to understand why we wanted to go to the platform above even though none of the shops there were currently open. By the time we finally burst out of the lift, my heart was racing. My fangs were fully extended, ready to rip into whoever had taken our Trish.

I checked my communicator. "Five life signs further ahead. One of them human."

We ran as fast as we could, Xil in the lead, Matar and I flanking him. Matar's tail was wrapped around his waist so as not to get in the way, but I knew he'd use it to fight our enemies as soon as we got close. The three of us had trained together. Yes, we'd been traders before we'd started our Alien Abduction for Beginners course, but that didn't mean we didn't know how to fight. On Kardar, every youngling learned how to defend themselves. Hatcheries taught combat skills in addition to academic subjects. With three sentient species living on the same planet, there had been many wars in the past. Right now, an unsteady peace kept everyone in check, but I was sure that one day, Kardarians would have to fight again.

The platform lay deserted, only a few lamps illuminating our path. Empty stalls, the tables covered in grey fabric, gave it a ghostly feel. Dust covered the ground. I didn't know why this platform was no longer used, but it was the perfect hideout for whoever had stolen Trish from us. It was lucky the elevator warden had agreed to take us here. Involving the station security would have taken way too long.

We sprinted in silence, faster than we'd ever run before. Finally, a silver pod glinted in the distance. My fangs poked my bottom lip as adrenaline pumped through me. Battle lust threatened to overwhelm me even though we hadn't even seen the abductors yet.

While running, I took a look at the communicator again. The life signs were moving away from us, but we were faster. It wouldn't be long before they came into sight.

Beside me, Matar was breathing hard, and I felt exhaustion creep up on me, too. None of us did much exercise. Now I regretted that. We'd done some weightlifting before we'd abducted Trish - the course had recommended for us to look our best so to attract our female - but that was a while ago now. I swore I would do regular cardio as soon as we were safely back on the Jade.

Finally, four figures came into view. Large, bulky, bipedal. It was too dark to see much more than that. I increased my speed even further. They weren't going to get away. One of them carried something on his shoulders. Trish?

"Ari, dial Trish," I commanded my communicator. I usually preferred manual input, but I wanted to keep my eyes on the abductors.

A traditional Kardarian folk dance started playing in front of us. Yes, they had Trish with them. I was glad I'd already set up her communicator.

"Stop!" Xil roared as soon as we got close enough for them to hear us.

They didn't even turn around, just kept running. Where were they even going? There was nothing up here. If they wanted to take them to their ship, they'd have to use one of the elevators, but they'd passed two of them already without stopping. Not that I wanted them to take a lift. I wasn't sure if the warden had alerted security. There was no time to check.

Once we got closer, I finally recognised the aliens. Tarpartians. Yuck. Since they hadn't actually developed spaceflight yet, there weren't many of them. They had the advantage of their planet having an extraordinarily strong gravitational pull, which had led many a spaceship to crash land on Tarpa. Scavenging parts and repairing ships, they'd somehow managed to reach nearby space stations. While they weren't very bright, they'd soon become known to be excellent bodyguards. They were loyal, tough, greedy and lacked morals. They'd do pretty much anything for the right incentive, like abducting a human. I doubted it was them who'd had the idea. They were just lackeys for whoever had really orchestrated the kidnapping. Had this been random or had they wanted Trish for some reason? In most places, humans weren't known at all since the only ones travelling the galaxy were those who'd been abducted. Peritus was making its first small steps towards the stars, but it would still take a while for them to be able to reach their closest planets, let alone a space station like Kitt-Y-6.

No, it had to have been random. That changing room had been a trap for the first person to step into it.

"Stop right now!" Xil bellowed once more.

The Tarpartians didn't care. Luckily, they were

slower than us. They were about our height but had a lot more bulk. And I wasn't talking about just muscles. Their body fat index had to be through the roof.

Just when we got close enough to launch our attack, they turned around as one, guns drawn, pointing right at us. Trish was slung over the shoulder of the tallest Tarpartian, struggling against his grip.

"Don't worry, Trish," I called out to her, and she lifted her head. Her hair was dishevelled and her eyes were rimmed with red, but otherwise, she seemed unharmed.

"Thank A'Ta," Matar exclaimed under his breath.

Even though I didn't believe in the deity, I felt the same relief. Now we just had to deal with the guns. We carried no weapons, so we had a problem. Not one I couldn't solve though. They were basic beta-laser-guns, the cheapest on the market. Perfect. Without taking my gaze off them, I typed into my communicator. I'd practised this so often I could do it in my sleep.

"Leave," the Tarpartian carrying Trish burped. Yes, he burped. It was how Tarpartian language sounded to anyone who wasn't a native speaker. Our translators turned it into actual words, but while the translation was delivered right into my brain, I could still hear their burping. It was disgusting. Probably one of the reasons why nobody wanted Tarpartians anywhere near them if they could help it. Unless of course you needed a scrupulous bodyguard. I assumed most people hiring them told them not to speak if it could be avoided.

"Return our human," Xil snarled. "She's ours."

"Not anymore," the grey alien burped. His mouth was so large that it created an echo chamber for the sound.

"What do you want with her?" I asked, playing for time. I still needed a moment to work on my communicator.

"None of your business," the Tarpartian on the right burped. "Now run off before we shoot you."

I pressed the final button and coughed, signalling Xil and Matar. The deed was done.

"Then shoot us," Xil grinned. "What are you waiting for?"

"No!" Trish shouted and struggled even harder. I hope she didn't hurt herself trying to get away from her captor. She had no chance of escaping his grip, as much as it pained me to admit that. Maybe we should teach her some self-defence skills. It wouldn't help her much when confronted with a burly Tarpartian, but it might aid her in less dangerous circumstances. You never knew what deranged aliens who might encounter in space.

The Tarpartians looked at each other.

"She told us not to harm them," the male carrying Trish muttered, barely loud enough for my translator to pick up his words.

"We should have taken stun guns," the one on the left whispered, and I realised it was a female. She looked exactly like the males, only her voice was slightly softer and her mouth smaller. Her burps were just as disgusting, though.

"I'm sure she won't mind if we kill them. She's only interested in the female," the Tarpartian who'd threatened us said.

"Come on, shoot us," I shouted. "Stop wasting our time!"

"What are you doing?" Trish screamed. "Are you insane?"

I wished I could have told her what was going on, but there was no way to safely do so. In fact, her panic helped us. The Tarpartians didn't suspect a thing.

"Fire on my command," the largest one burped.

I turned to Xil and Matar and gave them a wink, just in case. Everything was going to be fine.

"This is your last chance-"

"Just klatting do it," I interrupted him. "This is getting dull."

I forced myself to take on a relaxed, almost bored posture.

The Tarpartian snarled and pointed his gun right at me.

"I warned you..." he burped and fired.

Except that nothing actually happened. He stared at his gun and pressed the trigger once more. Nothing.

Xil roared and launched himself at the closest Tarpartian. Matar and I followed suit, using their distraction to attack. Before he could react, I reached the one on the right and plunged my fangs into his fleshy neck. I didn't have any venom, not like other fanged species, but that didn't matter because I hit an artery and blood poured into my mouth. I pulled back and spat out the sour blood, before kneeing him in the groin. He went down, clutching his neck, looking at me in shock. I wasn't sure if this would be enough to make him bleed out - I'd never fought a Tarpartian before - but for now, he was down.

"Havel, take Trish!" Xil commanded, and I didn't hesitate.

The male who'd been carrying her had simply dropped her on the floor to defend himself. Idiot. I ran to her side and scooped her into my arms before running away from the battle.

"Are you alright?" I demanded more harshly than I'd intended. "Are you hurt?"

"I'm fine, thanks to you. They didn't hurt me. Said their employer didn't want me harmed."

I growled. As soon as she was safe, we'd go after that employer. One of the Tarpartians had said that it was a female. That made it even more mysterious. A male may have wanted Trish as his human sex slave, but it was unlikely that a female would desire the same. Of course, some females preferred their own sex, but why choose a human?

We reached the closest elevator and the doors slid open. As soon as we were inside, I pushed the button, locking us in. No warden waited for us; the spot in the centre where they usually hovered was empty. Maybe this elevator shaft wasn't used anymore. I didn't care. We were safe now.

I set Trish down to inspect her, just in case she was injured after all. They'd bound her hands with wire, but it didn't take me long to get it off her. As soon as her arms were free, she clung to me. I held her tight, breathing in her scent, feeling her press against my body. Only now did the shock of almost losing her sink in.

"Trish," I whispered, but then there was no more time for words. I captured her lips and kissed her like I was starving. She cupped my face and locked me in place, returning the kiss just as passionately. She tasted sweet and spicy at once, even better than piki cakes. Her tongue swiped against my fangs, and I realised they were still more extended than they should be. I concentrated and slowly retracted them until just the tips poked out between my normal teeth. I didn't want to hurt her.

I held her, vowing to never let her go again. I was going to get a leash and keep her by my side, not letting her out of my sight. She was too precious to endanger. We should never have left her alone. From now on, one of us would always be with her. Especially until we knew who'd wanted to abduct her.

My communicator beeped. It had to be the others. I realised they wouldn't know where we'd disappeared to. Without breaking the kiss, I pushed the button to take the call.

But it wasn't my friends who spoke.

"Congratulations, you've passed the test."

I was going to kill her.

LESSON 5

NEST BUILDING FOR DUMMIES I

TRISH

I glared at the Professor, still not quite able to believe it had all been her doing. We were back on the Jade's bridge, all huddled together. I was on Xil's lap, but Havel had his hand on my thigh, and Matar leaned against me, his head on my shoulder. They'd not let go of me on the way here. Even while I'd showered and changed clothes, Xil had been with me. If Professor Katila hadn't been waiting for our call, I knew we'd be in bed now, all of us, claiming each other.

The shock still sat deep in my bones. Even now that I knew it hadn't been real, I was still on the verge of having a nervous breakdown. While I'd been carried off by that alien, I'd not allowed my fear to take hold of me. Now, it was close to overwhelming me. Only the guys' touch kept me from falling apart.

"You have done extremely well," Professor Katila said, giving us a smile. Bitch. "Top marks for all of you. Of course, you need to write a full report for our case study, but there's no doubt about your grade. You didn't hesitate once you found out your abductee had disappeared. You wasted no time in following her. I expected you to contact security or find some weapons, but I liked your method of disabling the Tarpartians' guns even more. Very effective. I also appreciate that you didn't kill them. I'd planned for that possibility, of course, but it does save me some paperwork."

"Why did you do that?" I accused her. "Do you have any idea how scary that was?"

She ignored me and looked at Xil instead. "You have proven excellent leadership. I might invite you to record a presentation on how you trained your team."

"I didn't train them," he said in a quiet, dangerous tone. "We grew up together. We had the same teachers. And if you were here right now, I'd show you some of the techniques they taught us."

Professor Katila didn't react to the threat. "As I said, I require a full report. That was your first practical assessment of this course, a second will follow soon. You'll have some time to prepare for that one."

"How generous," Matar huffed.

"Next, I'd like you to look after your female. She's been through quite a lot and needs to be reassured that she's safe with you. I've uploaded some presentations and readings on nest building for you."

I stared at her. "Nest building? Humans don't build nests."

Her third eye looked straight at me, making a shiver run down my spine. Her normal eyes were fixed on the guys, looking at each one of them in turn.

"You might want to get some building supplies from the space station while you're still there. Turn your bedroom into the ideal breeding environment. You'll want soft, warm colours, lights that can be dimmed, lots of pillows and soft furnishings. You already have a large enough bed, but maybe invest in a better mattress. You-"

"I don't need a nest and I don't breed," I hissed. I wanted to throw something at her, something sharp and dangerous.

"You may change your mind," she said, completely ignoring my protest. "Besides, Kardarians build nests, and we wouldn't want to deprive your males of that."

I looked at the guys. All three had murderous expressions painted across their faces. If Katila had been on the ship with us, she'd be dead by now.

Somehow, I doubted this arrangement would last much longer. How desperate were the guys to get their qualification? Now that they had me, they weren't' going to abduct anyone else. I was their one and only abductee. They were planning to go back to being traders again once they'd completed this course. Maybe I could convince them to do it sooner rather than later. Professor Katila gave me the creeps. I wouldn't have been surprised if she had more plans for my guys. And me.

"You have two days to complete this lesson," she continued. "Then we will have a debrief. I'll send you the time once I've squeezed you into my calendar."

She made it sound as if we should be grateful that she took the time for us. Urgh. What a bitch.

I breathed a sigh of relief when the screen went black. The only good thing about this conversation was that she'd distracted me from my fear.

Xil pressed a kiss on my shoulder. His lips were softer than ever. Yummy.

"We'll figure it out," he said soothingly. "I won't forget what she did to you. We'll make her pay for it."

The other two nodded.

"I don't care about that certificate," Matar growled. "She harmed our mate. There's no way I'm letting her get away with that."

"We," Havel corrected. "*We* will punish her."

Relief flooded me. I'd know they'd put me first, but it was good to hear how they were no longer motivated to complete their alien abduction course.

"Are you really going to build me a nest?" I asked them. "Humans don't have nests. Chickens, yes. Humans, no."

"Yes, we shall make you a nest, my little chicken," Xil laughed. "Whatever that may be."

I groaned. "A chicken is a bird, not a term of endearment."

"I think it sounds cute," Havel said, and I knew I'd made a mistake. From now on, I was going to be their chicken.

"Do Kardarians have nests?" I asked.

"We do. Males build them for their females as proof of their love and devotion," Matar explained. "They can take many shapes and forms. It's mostly a space for the couple - or multiple mates - to withdraw to. Somewhere to feel safe and at home. Unlike for egg-laying species, a nest isn't for incubating younglings. We use it to increase the bond between mates."

"And to breed," Xil added with another laugh. "That's why she suggested a better mattress."

I had to admit, I had no issue with more sex. After what we'd been through, I wanted them to hold me. To merge with me. To become one. It was the ultimate feeling of safety when I was in their arms. Nothing could harm us while we were together.

"I still find it weird," I admitted. "Nest sounds so... alien."

Matar snorted. "Glad you're only now noticing how you're an alien."

"You're the aliens," I shot back. "Humans are the centre of the universe."

"Of course they are," Havel said mildly. "Now you stay here with Xil or Matar while I start making that nest for you. We can order materials from the station without having to go outside again. They'll be delivered straight to the Jade."

"Can't I help?"

"No. Nest building is a task for us to do to honour our mate. But if you want, you can watch Katila's lesson about it and tell us the gist of it, just in case she asks us questions." I could hear him rolling his eyes without turning my head. "Every Kardarian male knows how to make a nest for their female. It's preposterous that she even sent us a presentation on it."

"I'll need snacks. Have the piki cakes arrived yet?"

The guys laughed. The sound dispelled all remaining anxiety, and I finally felt warm again. I was ready to forget about today's nightmare and move on to new, strange things. Like a nest.

. . .

In the end, all three of them disappeared, leaving me on the bridge with a piki cake and something resembling a smoothie. As much as I liked popcorn when watching films, this was even better. The cake dissolved in my mouth, letting flavours explode with every bite. I no longer cared what it was made of. All I cared about was knowing that we had lots of them stashed in the galley kitchen.

Instead of Professor Katila, another alien appeared on the screen when I started the pre-recorded lesson. I thought I'd seen some of his kind on the space station, but I didn't know the name of his species. He reminded me of a red frog with bulbous eyes, an enormous mouth and something like gills on his neck. His teeth were sharp, turning him from a harmless frog into a predator. He wore a toga-like robe, hiding most of his body. Only one arm was visible, making me curious how many limbs he was hiding beneath the toga.

"Welcome to this lesson," he said with a surprisingly soft voice. "Today we'll be discussing the traditional art of nest building. While all species have their own techniques, many share a common basic concept that we'll look at in detail. We will also examine why nests are the way to your female's heart or hearts and how you can use them to strengthen your bond. In the final part of the lesson, we will cover incubating eggs. If you belong to a species who doesn't lay eggs, you're allowed to skip that."

I was grateful for that. Although it might be fun to

find out more about aliens who laid eggs. I couldn't imagine having an egg inside of me... but as the guys continuously pointed out, humans were just one of many species in the universe. The aliens I'd seen on the shopping platform had mostly been bipedal and breathed oxygen, but that's because we hadn't been on any of the other platforms. Xil had explained that there were various platforms depending on customers' needs, whether they needed water to swim in, nitrogen to breathe, lower gravity or other requirements. It would have been fun to take a look at some of those, but then, I wouldn't have been able to survive there without some sort of spacesuit.

I focused on the teacher again. I realised he'd never introduced himself. Maybe he'd done other lessons before and assumed students would know his name. For now, I decided to call him Professor Frog. Was that speciest?

"A nest is the ultimate expression of safety and comfort. It's the centre of your home, where you and your mates will be intimate. I don't just mean physical intimacy. In a nest, it is a common rule to be completely honest with each other. A space of truth and love." He smiled and I despite his teeth, he looked happy and benign.

"Materials used to build nests depend on what you can find on your home planet. Some species will weave branches and other organic materials. My own kind uses algae and our parents' dried excrements to form the perfect nest. As I can't cover every single species in this lesson, I challenge you to look up your own traditions in the handbook I've attached."

A bing sounded, and a holographic book hovered above my communicator. Havel must have linked it to the Jade already. I had no idea what to do, so I simply pretended it was a real book and opened it. Even though my fingers didn't touch the virtual pages, the communicator seemed to recognise my movement and flicked to the first page. Although I was sure that was just for me, the book was written in English. I bet it didn't take the shape of a book for everyone either. Was that the Jade's AI's doing or something within the communicator? I'd have to ask the guys.

A table of contents showed a long list of different species.

"Pause the lesson," I said, and Professor Frog froze on the screen. I was much more interested in what I'd find out in the book than what he had to say. I clicked on Kardarians and the book's pages magically flipped to the corresponding chapter. I felt a bit like a wizard. Harry Potter, watch out, there's a new mage in town!

I skimmed the chapter, skipping the bits I already knew about Kardarians. My mates had told me how they were one of three species on their planet, that they had a variety of bright skin tones, that they had various features like fangs, tails, pointy ears and even claws. It didn't mention two cocks, but maybe that was too specific. I'd never asked Xil if he was an anomaly or if it was common among Kardarians to have more than one dick.

Kardarians use the highest quality materials they can afford. Utilising local materials is frowned upon and items from other planets is preferred. The more exotic, the better. Often, the parents of the male/males will add something from their own nest, like a pillow or blanket. Sometimes, the female's father will cover the nest with his scent to warn the males that they'll have to answer to him should they mistreat their mate.

I cringed at that. Thank goodness that wasn't an issue for me. If my males mistreated me - not that they ever would - I'd deal with them myself. No father needed and especially not his scent. Yuck. I wondered if the guys' parents would give me something for our nest once I met them.

I took one more bite of cake and continued reading.

Kardarian nests are comparatively small. They will fit the female and her mate or mates, but there's no space for furniture, offspring or other relatives.

Wait, relatives? Why on Earth would I want my relatives to be in a nest with me? That was weird. Were they supposed to watch while I slept with my guys? No way. I was surer than ever that I was lucky with my choice of mates.

While Kardarian males will take their female's opinion into account, they are very protective about their responsibility of building the perfect nest. They will continue to improve it until their female is completely satisfied. Once the nest is ready, they will mate in it repeatedly, often for several days, until the nest has taken on their scent. It's a way to stake their territory and show that they're a good match with their female.

Sex for days? Wow. Warmth pooled between my legs at the thought of being in my mates' arms, having them claim me again and again, only taking breaks to sleep and eat. It was kind of hot. Although I'd need some time to recover afterwards. The guys were *big*, and I could only take them so often until I got sore.

I pulled my mind out of the gutter and focused on the book.

Nests will be remade from scratch after each birth of a youngling. They increase by size each time, and it is assumed that the dwelling the family inhabits will also become larger.

Each time? How many children did Kardarians usually have? I wasn't planning on having kids any time soon, especially not several of them. I wanted to explore the galaxy together with my mates and children would only get in the way of that. One day, we'd settle down and start a family, yes, but not now.

I skimmed the rest of the text where it went into more detail of building techniques and strategies. The guys weren't letting me help with the nest anyway, so no need for me to study that. I closed the holo-book and continued watching the lesson. As interesting as some of it was, I had trouble concentrating. I wanted to know what the guys were doing.

If I'd had another piki cake, I might have been able to control my curiosity and stay on the bridge. Since I'd finished mine, however, I paused the recording. It was time to see what they were up to. And try out the nest.

LESSON 6

NEST BUILDING FOR DUMMIES II

XIL

Three males building one nest was a bad idea. Each of us had different ideas on how best to do it. And while they usually accepted that I was in charge, today neither wanted to back down. We all wanted to impress Trish, but we couldn't agree on what she'd want.

"This is impossible," I sighed after comparing our notes. After the first argument had almost turned into a fistfight, I'd decreed that we'd each write down our plans for the nest. Now we had three entirely different suggestions. Klat. Maybe we should have watched the IGU lesson after all. It may have explained how to solve disagreements between mates.

"Should we ask Trish to decide?" Havel asked, looking just as defeated as I felt. I didn't want to fight my friends, but there was also no way I'd back down from my plans. They were the best. Trish would love it. She'd fall into my arms and onto my cocks as soon as she'd see my nest.

"Or we could build three different nests," Matar suggested. "Then she can choose which one she wants to spend the most time in."

"We don't have space for three nests," I snapped. "Nor the time. Our parking meter is almost expired, and we haven't even ordered all the supplies we need. Staying for a second parking period will be expensive."

"Are you saying you don't like spending money on our mate?" Matar teased.

I growled at the engineer. "You know that's not true. But I want to be far away from here before Professor Katila comes up with yet another way to distract us."

"Trish is on her way here," Havel announced. "I put a tracker on her communicator after the incident earlier."

"Does she know?" I asked.

"Not yet. I didn't want to freak her out. We don't need it on the Jade, but from now on, I always want to know where she is. I don't think my heart will survive another kidnapping."

I had to agree with him. "Let's keep it quiet for now. What else have you installed?"

"All the usual. I added a Kardarian dictionary and software to help her learn our script. The translator will let her communicate with our families when we return home, but she won't be able to read any signs."

"Good thinking. Not that we'll go back to Kardar any time soon, but better to be prepared. I think she'll enjoy the challenge. Did you also add the Peritan books we downloaded during our research phase?"

Havel nodded. "Those and some of their films. For entertainment, if we're ever busy."

"I'll never be too busy for her," Matar said, but he shut up when I shot him a dark look. As our engineer, he was responsible for keeping the Jade in shape. With me flying the ship, it was Havel who'd be most likely to spend time with Trish during difficult periods. Not that

I was planning to get into any space battles any time soon, but our bumpy ride to Kitt-Y-6 had shown how quickly a situation could escalate.

"I thought you'd have started by now," Trish said, stepping into the room.

"We've removed the furniture," I grumbled, aware that this wasn't going as planned. I didn't care about Professor Katila's grades anymore, but I didn't want to disappoint Trish. She deserved to be the happiest female in the galaxy.

"I can see that," she quipped. "Wasn't the bed supposed to stay?"

"We'll return that once we've decorated the floor and walls," Havel explained. "How was the lesson?"

Trish shrugged. "Quite enlightening. Is it true the father of the bride rubs his scent all over the nest?"

I exchanged a look with the guys. From the way she said that it was clear that she didn't approve.

"Sometimes," I hedged. "It's not necessary. Was the lesson about Kardarians in particular? Did they use us three as an example again?"

"No, but I was given a book that had a chapter on you. Well, your species. It said how important this ritual is for you, which is why I'm surprised that you're not finished yet. Or at least further than... this." She laughed. "Do you want me to build you a nest instead?"

"No," all three of us said, completely aghast. A female building her own nest? I'd never heard of such a travesty. It would make her males the laughing stock of the entire planet. And Kardarians loved to laugh about each other. We'd never hear the end of it.

"Then what's the problem?" Trish asked.

I sighed and pointed at our three holo notes. "We can't agree on a plan. We all have different ideas, and none of us wants to back down."

"That's kind of adorable. How about I pick and choose bits from each of those plans? I'll try and make it so each of you has the same amount of input. I don't want you to fight over this."

"That would be great," Havel nodded before I could say anything else. "If you open the menu on your communicator, you can open a blank sheet of holo paper. Then just drag and drop the parts you want."

He fiddled with his own communicator and all our notes transformed into strange scribbles. That had to be her human way of writing. It looked ugly.

Trish sat on the floor - we should have left at least a chair in the room - and started reading through our plans. There was nothing for us to do but wait.

I wasn't a patient male. In fact, waiting was torture. I sat by her side to peek at her notes, but she turned her back to me.

"Don't look until I'm done. And don't you dare try and influence me."

She knew me too well.

"I'll get us some snacks," Matar volunteered. I hoped he meant Piki cakes by that. We'd given one to Trish earlier but hadn't taken any for ourselves. I'd make sure that she got most of them, but an occasional treat for us males was fine, too. Right? Or was I supposed to save them all for our female? Maybe I should. Before the kidnapping, I may have asked Professor Katila about that, but no klatting way was I going to contact her now.

My communicator pinged, signalling our time on Kitt-Y-6 was almost over. I suppressed a scowl and paid for a second parking period. We still hadn't ordered any supplies besides some basic pillows. Those wouldn't do for Trish's nest. Plus we needed to stock up on more food and fuel. In all the excitement earlier we'd lost track of those essentials. Shopping with Trish hadn't been the only reason we'd come to the space station.

I occupied myself by scrolling through the station's virtual catalogue, adding supplies to my basket. They'd be delivered to our ship before we left. At least now that I'd paid for a second parking period, we wouldn't have to pay a surcharge for fast delivery. And maybe... yes, we should take Trish to a restaurant. If she wasn't too scared to set foot outside the Jade again. I wouldn't think any less of her for that. It was a sign of her inner strength and resilience that she was sitting here with a smile on her face despite the ordeal she'd gone through just a few hours ago.

Just in case, I reserved us a table at the Outer Ring Restaurant. I'd never usually go there - it was way too expensive - but Trish deserved to be spoiled.

. . .

By the time Matar returned with Piki cakes and a tray of fresh fruit, I'd finished ordering supplies. Now, all we had to do was get the items we needed for our nest.

"I'm done," Trish announced and looked up from her note, smiling happily. "How do I translate this back into Kardarian?"

Havel reached out and touched her holo paper, flicking it to his own communicator. As soon as it landed there, it turned into our own alphabet. He sent copies to Matar and me, and we studied what Trish had compiled.

"Perfect," Matar exclaimed. "I think this is better than any of our plans."

Trish grinned. "Sometimes, it takes more than just the sum of the parts. Do I get some cake as a reward now?"

Faster than she could see, I grabbed her and pulled her against me, pressing my lips to hers. I kissed her passionately, hoping she'd understand how much I admired her. Loved her. She was the best mate I could have ever imagined.

"Xil, stop it," Havel said with a fake sigh. "You're the one who has to authorise the purchase. Go and order everything so we can get started on building the nest."

Instead of ending the kiss, Trish wrapped her arms around my back and clung to me. No way was I going to stop now. My cocks grew hard as her body moulded against me, a perfect fit. Our tongues danced, and it felt like our very first kiss once again. Every kiss with her was a new experience. It got better every single time, even though that was impossible. Our first kiss had been amazing, so how could it get even better?

Finally, I pulled away, breathless. Her eyes were wide, her lips swollen. I loved that look on her.

"Just send the klatting order," Matar said and pulled Trish to her feet, away from me. I immediately grew cold where she'd touched me. Being without her was like a brooding emptiness took over my heart, reminding me of how it had felt to almost lose her. It had been the worst moment of my life when I'd realised she'd been taken. I never wanted to feel anything like that ever again.

I quickly submitted the order, then snatched a piece of cake. If I couldn't have Trish, then I'd eat the second-best thing. As soon as we had our nest, I'd taste her, too. She loved it when I was between her legs, letting my tongue explore her most secret places. I enjoyed making her gasp with pleasure, have her grasp my head to prevent me from moving away.

"It won't be long before we get everything delivered," I told the others. "But I still want to build the nest without you watching, Trish. I know you've seen the plans, but I need it to be a surprise. It's tradition for the female to only see the nest once it's completed."

"I understand. I'll go and play with the tribitt," she said. "Hopefully he's done napping by now."

When we'd pursued her kidnappers, Matar had thrust the little animal at the stall owner. Luckily, it had still been there when we returned. I wasn't sure if the Brontes had been involved in Professor Katila's plot, but I hadn't trusted him one bit.

I watched as she left the room, a little sad that I couldn't go with her. But we had to build a nest. I looked back at the plans. We were going to have to hurry up or we'd never finish this today.

TRISH

The tribitt - I still hadn't decided on a name - was exhausted by the time the guys called me. We'd played for hours, and I'd started to get a good idea of the little space bunny's abilities. He was intelligent, and it shouldn't be too hard to teach him some tricks. The tribitt used his ears to communicate his mood. Hanging down was sad or tired, up straight seemed to be excited and him flicking them in my face was his way of telling me that he wanted food. Plus, a growl coming from his belly.

He also squeaked occasionally, and when I scratched him between his ears, he did something resembling a purr. It was the cutest sound ever.

Using my new communicator, I'd read up on tribitts and now knew that they ate almost anything. Very handy. I'd grabbed some stuff from the kitchen, and he'd scoffed down everything I gave him with no apparent preference for this or that. It would make feeding him easy. We could give him leftovers from meals without having to buy tribitt food. If that even existed.

The guide also mentioned that tribitts could get aggressive towards strangers, so I would make sure he'd cuddled with all the guys at least once. Although it would be fun to see the little green animal attack one of my mates. Would they fight back or simply let it happen?

I sat him into his bed, which was basically a large pillow I'd found in the cargo bay, and kissed him on his forehead. The tribitt yawned without opening his eyes. I smiled. Despite everything that had happened on the station, our shopping trip had been worth it.

I left him to sleep in peace and headed to the main bedroom. I had to admit I was a little nervous. The guys could be... intense when it came to their traditions. I sniggered when I remembered the first probing. They'd been so eager and at the same time terrified to make a mistake. By now, they'd accepted that we were all learning together, that it didn't have to be perfect the first time round - and that they weren't ever going to probe me again. One time had been enough, especially when knowing that they'd done a report about it for Professor Katila. She knew everything about our love life, and I hated that. Once we were done with the whole nest thing, I'd have to talk to the guys about perhaps dropping the IGU course. They'd be most willing to do so while the memory of my abduction was still fresh in their minds. And mine.

I shuddered and pushed that thought away.

Havel waited outside the bedroom, brimming with excitement.

"You're not allowed to enter until they give me the blue light."

"Blue? On Earth... Peritus it would be a green light."

"I'm blue, so it's a blue light," he said simply, as if that explained everything. "Did you have fun with the tribitt?"

Before I could answer, the door slid open. Xil and Matar stepped into the corridor.

"We're ready," Xil announced in a strangely sombre tone. "Tradition bids us to let you enter the nest first and arrange it to your liking. If there's anything that you don't like, remove it. Then... ehm..."

"Strip naked," Matar interrupted with a wide grin. "We'll join you as soon as we get changed into our ceremonial outfits."

I was starting to realise that this was an even bigger deal for them than I'd thought, even after reading the lesson and reading the chapter on Kardarians. I guessed I wasn't used to them being so flustered and solemn.

With a nod, I squeezed past them into the room. The previously bright lamps embedded in the ceiling had been covered with red fabric, dimming the light but also reminding me of a brothel. Probably not what they were going for. The walls were hidden behind more fabric, black and more dark red. It made the room seem smaller, more intimate. But yes, definitely a brothel.

The guys had removed all furniture, even the bed frame. Instead, ten large mattresses, twice as wide as our original one, throned on top of each other in the centre of the room surrounded by hundreds of pillows. Not kidding. I wasn't going to count them, but there had to be at least a hundred pillows of various sizes. They ranged from cushions like you'd have on your sofa to fluffy monstrosities almost as long as me. Wow. They were mostly black, with some red and purple to make it look less like a funeral pyre. That's what it was. A pillow pyre.

I stifled a laugh just in case they were outside, listening to my reaction. They'd clearly put a lot of work and effort into this.

The mattress was covered in shimmering black fabric, similar to silk but with more sparkle. I ran my hand over it. Cool, yet soft. I bet it would feel amazing to have it against my naked skin. Of course, I'd find out soon enough.

I slipped out of my clothes in record time and threw them into a corner. It felt a bit weird to be naked without the guys in the same room. Hopefully, they'd join me soon. I made my way through the pillow mountains. Something hot hit my foot, and I suppressed a shout of surprise. Didn't want the guys to come in guns blazing. Rummaging around the cushions, I searched for whatever I'd stepped on. It was a stone, smooth and grey and very warm. A strange scent hit my nostrils and I gave it an experimental sniff. Yes, the stone was giving off a calming scent that I couldn't quite identify. Not flowery, more like smoke and spices. It made me think of a cold winter's night, sitting in front of a fireplace, wrapped in blankets, surrounded by my mates. I closed my eyes and breathed in the scent. It made me feel at home.

Of all the things in this nest, this was the best part so far. Maybe I judged a little too quickly. Were there any other surprises hidden beneath the pillows?

I put the stone on the bed, then went on my hands and knees to search. My fingers clasped around something hard and coarse. It felt like a branch or stick, but I couldn't dislodge it. I threw some of the pillows hiding it aside until I saw the strange item. It was twice as long as my arm and looked like a dried snake, with a thin body and round ends. Not kidding. *Please, don't let this be some kind of aphrodisiac food that I'll have to eat.* It didn't feel organic, though, more like pottery or stone. I'd break my teeth trying to eat it. One end of the almost-snake was screwed to the floor, which is why I hadn't been able to lift it. Curious. I'd have to ask the guys about it. Unless it was an oversized sex toy, I couldn't imagine it's purpose.

I covered it under pillows again - just in case it was a sex toy that they wanted me to fuck - and searched the other side of the room for more surprises. I found a pile of yellow leaves that smelled like vanilla and two more of the hot stones. They were smaller than the one I'd stepped on but had the same beautiful scent. I added them to their sibling on the bed. I wanted to have them close, not buried beneath cushions.

A knock on the door made me whirl around.

"Are you ready for us to come in?" Xil called.

I quickly jumped on the mattress - which erupted into fireworks. What the fuck. I gasped as colours spread over the black fabric where I'd touched it. It was like rainbows surrounding me, trapped in the material but close to bursting out of it. I'd never seen anything like it. This had to be some kind of technology, but the sheets were thin like silk, so how did it work? Where was the power source? Not that it mattered. I didn't really care how it did what it did. I slowly moved my hand over the bed and marvelled at the colours exploding into life. Sparks seemed to fly through the air, even though I knew they were inside the fabric. Beautiful.

I lay on my back, naked and surrounded by swirling colours, and told the guys to enter.

LESSON 7

BREEDING FOR ADVANCED BEGINNERS

MATAR

My breath caught in my throat as I stepped into the room.

She was perfect.

Trish was spread out on the bed, her legs slightly parted, her nipples hard, her cheeks flushed. Her belly still wore the signs of our first mating: blue, yellow and green. She was ours. And she was ready to be bred.

I was rock hard already, and I hadn't even touched her yet. Luckily, the ceremonial breeding garment was designed with precisely that in mind. Instead of trousers, I wore a loose-fitting kilt. Beneath it, I was bare. My chest was covered in paint, the traditional symbols of my family and clan. Since we'd grown up in the same community, Xil and Havel had the same symbols except for two each that represented our parents. On our backs, we'd added our own sign, one we'd designed yesterday without Trish's knowledge. It would be our family's mark, to be passed through the generations from this point on.

"You look amazing," Trish gasped. "I never knew you guys had kilts. You look so Scottish, well, alien-Scottish."

I didn't ask her what that meant. The time for talking was over.

Before I joined her on the bed, I quickly looked around the room. She'd not removed anything. That meant she liked our arrangement. In the end, we'd decided to keep it simple, foregoing a lot of the ideas we'd had. It had felt wrong for Trish to know what we were planning, even though it had been helpful to have her mediate. We'd paired it all back to the bare essentials, making the room cosy, warm and comfortable. Since we'd only used a small part of our budget, Xil had splashed out on the most luxurious Lap'tan sheets. The expense had been worth it for seeing her on them. It was like she was lying on a galaxy.

She'd taken the fire stones and arranged them on the bed. Those had been my idea. We'd always had some of those in my family home and they reminded me of my childhood. I hadn't found any with the scents I was used to, but once we visited Kardar, I'd buy some of them. She seemed to like the stones, or she wouldn't have put them next to her.

Xil cleared his throat, and I realised I'd not taken my place by his side. It was time to begin the ritual. Now that we'd built the nest, we had to turn it truly ours. Mark it with our scents and memories.

"We have built a nest to honour you," Xil began the speech that males had recited during the breeding ceremony for generations. "As our mate, you have secured your place in our hearts, in our minds and our home."

"You're in my heart, my mind, my home," Havel said solemnly before I repeated the same words.

"This nest is the symbol of what we pledge to you," Xil continued. "We shall keep you safe. We shall keep you warm. We shall keep you happy. And we shall keep you satisfied."

That was the signal to lift our kilts, revealing our erect cocks. I didn't have to look at Xil and Havel to know they were just as aroused as I was.

"Wow," Trish muttered before quickly covering her mouth with her hands.

Slowly, Xil unbuttoned his kilt and let it drop to the floor. "We shall provide you with our seed of life. We shall care for the offspring that we will create together. We pledge to keep harm from our family until the day we die."

"Until the day we die," Havel and I echoed solemnly.

"Will you accept this nest?" Xil asked and stepped forward until his legs touched the mattress. "Will you accept us as your mates?"

Trish nodded. "I do."

She bit her bottom lip the way she always did when she was nervous or unsure. I had to remind myself that she didn't know this ritual. She had no idea what would come next. There was no right or wrong for her parts of the ceremony, though. While the males' words were set and couldn't be changed, the female could reply with whatever she wanted. I thought it was intentional to give the female the power over this rite.

"Will you accept our seed as a symbol of our love?" Xil asked, his gaze locked on Trish. I was jealous it was him to ask her first. Before meeting her, I hadn't minded at all that he was the Captain of the ship. Now that we had a mate, I didn't always find it easy to watch Xil in charge.

Trish did a choked sort of sound, but then rose to her knees until her mouth was almost level with Xil's cocks. She looked up at him with her beautiful wide eyes before taking his lower cock in her mouth. It wasn't part of the ritual, but it was perfect. My own cock ached, needing her touch. My tail wrapped around my thigh, even though it wanted to curl around Trish.

I almost drooled as I watched Trish take Xil's lower cock deep into her mouth while rubbing his upper cock with her nimble fingers. A thin line of drool ran down her chin, landing on her full breasts. I couldn't hold back any longer. I went on my knees next to Xil and gently put my hands on her hips, turning her ever so slightly towards me. I pulled her closer until I could kiss her naked belly. She gagged as Xil's cock pushed deeper into her throat, but the scent coming from between her legs made it very clear how much she was loving this.

I ran my tongue over her skin, slowly moving up until my head was between her breasts. Using my grip on her hips to keep her steady, I took one of her nipples into my mouth. It was hard and pebbled, perfect for suckling on. I sucked on her nipple as hard as I could without hurting her, relishing the way she moaned against Xil's cock. That was my doing, not his. I cupped her other breast with my hand and simply held it for a moment, admiring the weight. Her breasts were perfect. Everything about her was, but I could spend all day worshipping her boobs. I swirled my tongue around her nipple, causing her to arch her back and push against my face. She wanted more. Well, she only had to ask.

My tail uncurled from my leg and touched the inside of her thigh. With Xil's cocks blocking her view, she probably didn't know that it was my tail instead of my hand. I'd not dared introduce this to our mating until now, but today was special. Trish opened her legs, adjusting her position to give me access. Moisture glistened between her thighs, showing me exactly how ready she was for us. I'd enter her soon enough, but for now, my tail would give her the pleasure she deserved.

I moved it closer to her entrance, letting the tip run around her swollen sex, just about touching her. She quivered and tried to grind her hips against the tail, but I kept her locked in place, toying with her. I didn't give her the satisfaction of having my tail touch her where she really wanted to. I kept to the outer lips, smearing her juices all over her beautiful pussy, preparing her for me. For us. We were all going to take her, again and again. We wouldn't leave this nest until all four of us were sated, exhausted and carrying each other's scent. This breeding ceremony was the most important moment in a mate's relationship, and I was going to savour every single second.

Finally, I rubbed my tail's enlarged tip against her bud. She moaned against Xil's cock and her entire body shook. She was close to coming. I looked down at my own cock. So was I. If I drove into her now, there would be no holding back. But I was aware that Xil would be the first. Then Havel and I had to fight for second place. Where was that blue-skinned bastard? Without stopping my tail's slow circles around Trish's clit, I looked at my friend. He was still a few feet away from us, stroking his cock, his eyes glazed. He was enjoying the show. Good for him. I was more of a doer than a watcher.

"Please," Trish whimpered, breathing hard. "Fuck me."

"No," Xil growled. "I'm not going to fuck you. I'm going to *breed* you. I'm going to mark you. I'm going to fill you with my seed. And I'm going to make sure everyone knows you're mine."

A shiver ran down my back. That was hot.

"And then Matar and Havel are going to do the same. Breed you. Make you their mate. And once you've come again and again, milking our cocks, we're going to worship your body. We will show you how much we love and adore you."

I never knew he had it in him. That had been one poetic speech. Sexy. I was even hornier now, something I hadn't thought possible.

It was time to do something about that. Xil's would be the first cock to enter her, but nobody had mentioned anything about a tail. I flicked the tip of it against her clit one last time, then pushed into her in one hard stroke. She screamed in pleasure and bucked her hips against me. This time, I let her. I fucked her with my tail, wishing it was my cock. It wasn't quite as thick, but it was longer, and I could reach all the way into her depths.

"Klatting stop that," Xil snapped at me. "It's my turn."

With a whole load of regret, I pulled back and let go of Trish, joining Havel on the side-lines.

"Would you like one or both?" Xil asked our female. She didn't have to ask what he meant.

"Both."

Now I wished I'd prepared her little rosebud as well as her pussy. Too late. With Xil's large back hiding Trish from view, I couldn't see what he was doing, but I hoped he was using some of her moisture to get her ready for him. Xil's cocks were a little less thick than mine, but he had two of them to make up for that. Thankfully, this wasn't our first time with Trish, and she was used to our large alien cocks. She'd said that human males were less well endowed, which had flattered all three of us. We were above average for Kardarians as well, but it always felt good to be appreciated like that by a female.

With one hand, Xil positioned himself, then plunged into Trish with both cocks at once. She cried out and grabbed the bedsheet with her hands. Colours exploded all around her like fireworks as Xil started fucking her. It seemed the perfect metaphor for what was happening. Xil groaned in unison with Trish's moans, creating a song that I couldn't wait to join.

I stroked my cock, pretending my hand was Trish's tight pussy.

"Soon it's our turn," Havel whispered hoarsely. "You fuck her, I take her mouth?"

He surprised me, but I wouldn't turn down that offer. "Agreed. We shall fill her from all sides, in all her holes. She'll never want another mate ever again."

"I heard that!" Trish screamed. "And I will be yours, always."

I almost came at her words. I knew she meant it. She was ours. Our mate. To be loved, cherished and fucked.

Xil breathed hard as he pummelled into her. The sound of his balls slapping against her skin echoed through the room.

"I'm close," he groaned. The muscles in his arse were tight, and I knew I looked the same when I was on the last sprint, almost ready to spill myself within her.

"Then come in me," Trish begged. "I want to come with you."

"You shall." He reached around, probably to rub her clit while continuing to fuck her in deep, hard strokes. I had to admit, it was more than hot watching them from this perspective. Before, when we'd been with Trish all at once, we were usually on the bed, two of us caressing her while the third buried himself within her. Now, Havel and I weren't able to caress her skin. All we could do was watch as she exploded around Xil with a primal cry, at the same time as he pushed into her one last time, arching his back, filling her with his seed. A drop of precum dripped from my cock, landing on a random cushion. No matter. Soon, the entire nest would smell of our mating. That's what we'd built it for. And a proper breeding ceremony wasn't complete without our scent covering half the pillows.

Xil bent over Trish and kissed her. I gave my cock one last stroke, knowing it was my turn now. I waited until Xil pulled out of her and stepped aside, then there was no stopping me. Her pussy and arse were wide open, stretched by Xil's two cocks. Waiting for me.

I had no patience for foreplay. Been there, done that. I pressed my tail's tip against her tight arse and pushed against the resistance, snaking it into her dark tunnel. I twisted it from side to side, grinning with satisfaction when Trish's moans told me how much she enjoyed it. I'd never used my tail on other females in the past. It was something intimate, precious, and I'd waited for a mate like Trish to try it. The way my tail felt inside of her, the pressure her muscles put on me, it was a sensation unlike anything else. It was time to fuck her or I'd come before I'd even entered her.

"Ready?" I asked and met her beautiful eyes. She smiled at me, and that was all I needed.

I drove into her in one stroke. She was wet and eager, almost pulling me in. I bent over her until I could kiss her breasts, then sucked on one while slowly grating my hips against hers. I wanted it to last just a while longer. If I pummelled into her like Xil had, I'd come in an instant.

Her inner muscles seemed to milk my cock. I

matched her rhythm with suckling on her nipple, giving it a gentle squeeze with my teeth every time I pushed into her arse and pussy. I let my tail fuck her hard, pulling out almost entirely before diving in again, making her squeal every time the tip pushed past her tight entrance.

"Do it," Trish moaned. "Come in me. Breed me. Be my mate."

There was no holding back. Not any longer. I stood up straight, lifted her legs until my thighs were pressed against hers, and fucked her harder than ever before. It seemed like both an instant and an eternity until I came, shooting my seed deep into her. I screamed at the same time as her, then kept her screaming by fucking her with my tail. I kept my cock inside her, still hard, enjoying the sensation of feeling my own tail through her inner walls. I'd only need a short break before I could do this again. And then again. She was mine.

"My turn," Havel said and put a hand on my shoulder. "I've changed my mind. I need to fuck her in her pussy first before taking her mouth."

As much as I wanted to stay in her warm, dark caves, I knew it was time to relinquish my position.

I pulled out of her, kissed the sole of her foot simply because it was at the same level as my mouth, then gently lowered her legs until they dangled over the side of the mattress again. Only when I stepped back, I realised how exhausted I was. I supposed it wasn't just from this mind-blowing sex with Trish. No, she'd also been abducted, and we'd been shopping. Both of those would have been enough to make any male tired.

I lay down on her other side and slid an arm around her shoulders, supporting her while Havel took his place at her feet. Instead of fucking her right away, he went on his knees and licked her entrance, cleaning her. Maybe he wanted his scent to be the only one he could smell on her beautiful pussy. I didn't care. I closed my eyes, snuggled against my mate and just enjoyed her closeness. Her moans grew louder and more frantic. I almost felt guilty for relaxing while she was still in the throes of another oncoming orgasm. Her skin was hot and sweaty, just like my own. We'd all need a shower after this. If Xil hadn't booked us a table at some fancy restaurant, I would have voted for staying in our nest for the next few days. We'd only leave for food and the occasional shower. With Trish, of course. A shower without her pressed against my naked body wasn't worth it.

Just before Trish succumbed to Havel's skills with his tongue, he stood up. "I want you on all fours," he said hoarsely. "I want to take you from behind."

Trish shivered and her sweet aroma filled my nose. Her arousal was reaching new heights. She slowly turned onto her front and climbed to all fours. She had to be exhausted, but the thought of being taken by Havel like that seemed to be enough to give her new strength. Not that I knew what that felt like. I'd never been with a male.

Her breasts hung low, ripe for the picking. I twisted

a little until I could reach her perfect nipples. Realising what I wanted, she lowered herself just enough until her breasts touched my lips. I waited for the moment Havel entered her, then opened my mouth and sucked in her hard nipple. I vaguely felt Xil doing the same on her other side. We were latched onto her, holding her in place like Kardarian nipple clamps, until Havel came with a triumphant cry.

We ended up in a huddle on the soft mattress. It had stopped its colourful display and was now showing large streaks of paint instead. Blue, yellow and green, just like the cum stains on Trish's skin. We hadn't added any new ones today, but this was only the beginning. One day, she'd be covered in our colours.

"I never got to give you my present," Xil muttered sleepily.

"What is it?"

He chuckled. "You'll find out the next time we're in this nest. I promise."

"I'll hold you to that." I heard her smile in her voice, and I had to grin myself. She had no idea what she was in for.

LESSON 8

HOW TO BEHAVE IN A FORMAL SETTING

TRISH

I hadn't thought I'd want to set foot on Kitt-Y-6 again, but when Xil had suggested going to some fancy restaurant, I couldn't say no. A restaurant in space - I had to see that. Besides, Xil had looked so hopeful that it would have been cruel to deny him this pleasure.

After a quick shower, I met the guys by the airlock. They'd all dressed in their nicest clothes. Not all of them were to my taste. At some point, we'd need to have a chat about the state of their wardrobes. At least they hadn't cut holes into their trousers again. I chuckled to myself at the memory of their attempt at lingerie.

Since we'd never actually bought any clothes for me at that stall, I was in my usual attire, although I'd pinned up my hair with some chopsticks I'd found in the galley. Hopefully, the restaurant wasn't so posh that they'd not let us in. I assumed that every alien species had their own idea of what was formal and posh, so we could simply pretend that we were at the height of fashion.

"Our shuttle has arrived," Havel announced with a look at his communicator. "Right on time."

"Is it too far to walk?" I asked.

He laughed. "You couldn't walk there at all. The restaurant is in the outer ring that circles the main part of the space station. You only get there by shuttle or one of the service elevators, which we don't have access to."

I'd got a glimpse of the station's layout when we'd approached, but I'd still been nauseous after our bumpy ride and hadn't paid full attention to it. Two giant rings surrounded the long, oval station. I'd assumed they were just for keeping the station supplied with power or stuff like that. Never in a million years would I have expected a fancy restaurant to be in those rings.

Xil held out his arm. "According to the human videos we watched, you'll have to hold onto me," he explained. "You'll have to explain why, though. Are you unsteady on your feet before a *date*?"

He emphasised the last word as if it was something strange and peculiar to him.

I laughed. "You need to stop watching those videos. And no, I'm not unsteady. Look at my shoes. Do you see any high heels? No. So don't worry about that. But I'll take your arm anyway because I like touching you."

Xil wiggled his eyebrows. "I know. You did a lot of touching in our nest."

"So did you. All of you." I licked my lips. They still felt a little swollen.

"That was only the beginning," Matar whispered into my ear. His hot breath kissed my skin, and a pleasant shiver ran down my back, ending right between my legs. "When we're back, we'll return to our nest."

Havel stepped closer and ran his hand over my

bum. "We hadn't even reached the main course yet, little human."

I shivered and suddenly I was glad for Xil's support.

"If you continue like that, we'll never get to the restaurant," I huffed, but it was a weak protest. I had no issue with them taking me right here, ripping off my clothes, fucking me against the wall.

What was going on with me? I'd never been this horny before I was abducted. Now, I was like a dog in heat, always ready for their cocks.

"Yes, we better go," Xil said. The door slid open, revealing a sleek silver ovoid parked next to the Jade. It looked like it had been taken right out of a science-fiction movie. I rolled my eyes at myself. I was in *space* surrounded by *aliens*. I better get used to it.

A round door opened in the shuttle's wall and we stepped inside. There was just about enough space for the four of us. Even another woman my size would have been a tight squeeze. The silver walls were lined with benches topped with red velvet pillows. It looked like velvet, anyway. When I sat down, a seat belt appeared out of nowhere and snaked around my waist. I pulled on it just to see if it would open, but it stayed tight. I wasn't sure if I liked that. Being strapped into a shuttle without a way to free myself seemed daunting, especially after my earlier abduction. If Professor Katila somehow took control of the shuttle, we'd be defenceless.

The guys didn't seem to have any issue, relaxing

into their seats. The door closed without a sound, and we took off in one smooth motion. The walls that had been silver until now turned translucent, giving us a view of the spaceport.

The shuttle swerved around much larger ships, easily manoeuvring its way to the very top of the hangar. A hatch slid open, just big enough for the shuttle, and then we were back in the vacuum of space. There had to be some kind of invisible airlock to prevent the oxygen from escaping. Even though I'd seen lots of space in the Jade, being in such a tiny shuttle with windows all around me was different. This might be what it felt like to drift in the vast nothingness in just a spacesuit. I'd asked the guys about that, but they'd forbidden me from ever attempting that. They only ever went on a spacewalk for essential repairs, and all three of them hated it. Even lots of blowjobs wouldn't change their mind. And those worked to persuade them of almost anything.

The first ring came into view, slowly circling around the station. From up close, it was much bigger than it had seemed from the Jade. We flew alongside it, slowly and with occasional turns to let us see the ring from all sides. I was starting to suspect the shuttle was giving us a tour and not just a quick lift to the restaurant.

"The rings are quite an old-fashioned space station design," Matar said, breaking the silence. "Lots of station enthusiasts come here to see them up close."

Figured that there was an equivalent of railway fanatics.

"We should see the restaurant shortly."

I was glued to the windows, fascinated by the majestic turn of the rings. They reminded me of whales slowly moving through the depths of the ocean for some reason, not that it made any sense.

A neon sign attached to the outside of the ring caught my attention. Seriously? It looked like an American diner. That had to be the restaurant. I adjusted my expectations a little. Maybe not quite as posh as I'd imagined.

We landed just as smoothly as the take-off had been. The walls turned silver again before the door slid open.

"After you," Xil said, clearly trying out another line from some film. Goodness me, my aliens were adorable.

I climbed out of the shuttle, glad I didn't wear a skirt or dress.

A tall alien awaited us, towering even above my guys. I wasn't sure if they were male or female - they had a long beard decorated with tiny crystals as well as six teats on full display. The only clothing they wore was a flimsy loincloth. Their feet were furry and ended in thick black claws.

"Welcome to the Outer Ring Restaurant," they welcomed us in a deep voice that made me think of church bells ringing. "A reservation for four?"

"Yes, under the name of Xil of the Jade," the captain replied and held out his arm to me again.

I took it to keep him happy. The other two stood close to me, so close I felt their warmth.

"Follow me," the alien said and led us through an intricate metal gate, away from the shuttle and into the actual restaurant.

I gasped at the sight. Not a diner after all. Thousands of lights sparkled on the ceiling like stars, while every table had candles floating above it. The room was dark, but not gloomy, letting the candles and stars provide all the light. Small tables were scattered across the large room with enough space between them to give it an intimate feel. The floor was thick carpet that my feet seemed to sink into. And then there was the view. Windows reached all the way to the ceiling, offering us a breath-taking view of space to our left and the station to our right. The second ring, barely visible, rotated around the station. It seemed to move slower than this ring, but that may have been an optical illusion.

The waiter led us to a table on the left, hidden behind a wall of plants. It was the perfect spot. When I sat down, I couldn't see the rest of the restaurant, making it seem like we were alone with nothing but the vastness of space.

"This is amazing," I breathed, my heart beating faster. "I didn't think it would be this beautiful."

Havel pulled a chair out for me. I may have swooned a little. They were really trying to make this as perfect as possible. And as human. Next time, I'd ask them about Kardarian dating traditions, but for now, I'd just enjoy the evening.

"Menus will appear on your communicators," the waiter explained. "For now, here are some complimentary drinks, chosen by the AI cook based on your species, weight and pheromones."

My what?!

A tiny drone appeared above us, holding four glasses. What was the waiter for then? The menus and the food delivery was automatic, so why was there even a person?

The drone set the smallest glass in front of me, filled with what looked like apple juice. Or urine, but I didn't want to go there. The guys all had the same blue liquid in their glasses, but they varied in size. Matar had the biggest.

"I think there's a direct correlation between my glass and the size of my dick," he announced with a wide grin. "The AI seems to know its stuff."

Men. Always the same.

I held up my glass. "Cheers!"

The guys stared at me in confusion.

"Isn't cheers slang for 'thank you'?" Havel asked. "Are you thanking us for taking you here? Or the drone for delivering the drinks? Or the AI for choosing this drink?"

"No, I wasn't thanking anyone. It's what you say before you clink glasses."

"Clink?" Xil repeated. "I know Ankanis smash their

glasses together after they're done with their meal and then use the shards to carve their names into the table. They're not allowed into some restaurants because of that. Do humans conduct a similar ritual?"

I laughed. "No. Let's just forget it. What drink did they give you?"

Matar took a sip and a dreamy expression crept across his face. "Bandulan liqueur. This AI is klatting amazing."

"Can I try?"

"Better not. This stuff is strong. Maybe before we leave, that way you won't be drunk during the meal."

I was getting used to that. The guys had some beer-like alcohol on the Jade that I wasn't allowed to drink. Well, technically I was, but after the first time and the worst hangover in the history of mankind, I'd decided to stick to non-alcoholic beverages.

I tried my own drink. It was sweet but nothing like apple juice. Maybe if you mixed mirabelle plums with quince and bananas, you might get something vaguely resembling this concoction. No, scratch that. It was too alien to compare it to Earth tastes. But it was amazing. I emptied half my glass before remembering that we were supposed to look at the menu.

I activated my communicator with a flick of my wrist, and a holographic menu appeared right in front of me. The text - in English - was written on three sheets that seemed to compete at grabbing my attention. They moved from side to side, changing position, pushing in front of each other.

"The AI is trying to decide what you might like," Havel explained with a laugh. "Here, press that button and they'll freeze."

I did as he showed me and the menu turned still, giving me the chance to actually read it. Not that any of the dishes made sense to me. Lopus steak with iask leaves and quagbu gratin. How was I supposed to know which of these dishes were good, let alone safe to eat for humans?

"Are any of these things poisonous?" I quietly asked the guys.

Xil roared with laughter as if I'd made the biggest joke of the galaxy. I kicked him beneath the table, but Matar's pained gasp told me I'd missed. Oops.

"The menu only contains dishes that are agreeable with your species," Havel explained. He didn't laugh, which made him my favourite mate at this moment. "Once you've read through them all, you can activate the AI again, and it'll rank them by what it thinks you'll enjoy most. Of course, you may be the first human ever to eat at this restaurant, so I don't know how accurate it'll be."

I skimmed the menu, but it was pointless. Even though some words were translated into English, most didn't make any sense at all. Luckily, I was pretty easy with food. Living the way I had before the guys had abducted me, I'd been glad for any food I could get my hands on. I could be choosy when it came to exotic meats, though, which made me ask Havel if I could sort the dishes to only show vegetarian ones.

"Are you sure?" Xil asked, still chuckling. "Goo'on fowl is a delicacy."

"Thanks, but I think I'll stick to something veggie myself and then try some of yours."

"You can taste mine any time you like, sweetheart," Xil said in a low, sultry voice.

I hated that his words made my pussy throb with need. As if we didn't just spend hours in our nest. I should concentrate on the food. On the restaurant. And not on the extremely hot and horny guys surrounding me.

The waiter reappeared, saving me from responding to Xil's flirting.

"Have you chosen your meal yet?" they asked pleasantly. "If so, please press your choice on the menu and it will be brought to you momentarily."

They gave us a short bow and left without another word. Yeah, they were utterly useless. Nice, friendly, yes, but also not needed. Was this what Earth's restaurants would be like in the future? Automated except for a random waiter to greet you?

I didn't know if I'd ever find out. For now, returning to Earth wasn't on our agenda. There was nothing there for me, and I'd much rather explore other planets. Unless the IGU told my mates to return to Earth for some reason, I doubted we'd go back there again.

Havel helped me choose a vegetarian dish, then pressed a whole lot of things on his own menu. I'd not even considered having several courses. I'd grown up in poverty and wasn't used to splashing out food.

As soon as everyone had made their choice, the holo menus disappeared. I blinked, my eyes getting used to the dark again. The candles floating above us twinkled like stars, while also giving off a pleasant aroma.

"Do you like it here?" Matar asked me after a moment's silence.

"It's beautiful. Have you been here before?"

"Only me," Xil said. "With my father, when we still spoke to each other."

"He's loaded," Matar whispered. "One of the richest Kardarians out there."

"Doesn't matter," Xil said, steel in his voice. "Let's talk of better things. Like where we're going from here."

"Riva Four is beautiful at this time of year," Havel suggested. "The trees will be laden with fruit. As long as we don't expose ourselves to the locals, we could spend some time there. Our moon of honey."

It took me a moment to understand what he'd meant. "Honeymoon," I corrected him with a laugh. "And you only do that after you're married."

"Do you want to be?" Xil asked seriously. "Married? I've read about it. I thought mating would be enough, but we can do a marriage, too, if you'd like. And then we can go on the moo- honeymoon."

I thought about that for a moment. Did I want to get married? No, not really. I knew without a doubt that I loved my guys and that they loved me. They'd built me a nest, for fuck's sake, no sane person would do that unless they loved their mate. And we'd done their strange kilt ceremony. I licked my bottom lip. Those had been hot. I'd have to tell them to wear kilts more often. Like, all the time. With nothing underneath, obviously. I could educate them about the advantages of going commando, maybe even some practical exercises... they'd forget about Professor Katila very fast.

"No, we don't need to get married," I told them. "But you're right, that doesn't mean that we can't go on a honeymoon. Or simply go on holiday, all of us together. Our relationship is new. There haven't been humans with Kardarians before. We can pick and choose whatever traditions we want. So I say we take all the good stuff and ignore the boring or tedious customs."

"Cheers to that," Havel exclaimed and raised his glass just like I'd done earlier. He was a quick learner.

A buzzing sound made me look up to four approaching drones. This time, we had one each hovering above our heads before they slowly descended, setting their loads on the table. I waited before they'd buzzed off before inspecting my food. Well, I couldn't actually see any food. I'd been given an ovoid looking like a tiny version of the shuttle we'd arrived in.

"What is that?" I asked, staring at the metal pod. "Don't they have plates here?"

I'd assumed a plate was a universal thing. The guys had them on the Jade. Not round, square, but still the same concept as on Earth: a portable and washable surface for your food.

Xil laughed. "This place is too expensive for plates. Lay your hand on it and see what happens."

Luckily, Matar and Havel seemed just as confused.

With a shrug, I placed my hand on the ovoid, and it dissolved at the touch. Yes, it *dissolved*, raining down in tiny flecks, landing on my food. The bottom half of the pod stayed solid, now acting as a sort of bowl.

"Seasoning," Xil said as if that was entirely normal. "If you want more, just use your communicator to alert the waiter."

Okay then...

"What if I didn't want any seasoning?"

Immediately, all three guys looked at me with concern.

"You don't?" Xil asked. "We can get you a new portion without any."

"We'll complain to the cook," Havel added.

"They should never have done that without asking," Matar growled.

I couldn't help but laugh. And here I'd thought the tribitt was cute. My mates were on an entirely different level.

"Guys, it's alright, it was just a hypothetical question. Do we get cutlery or do we eat with our hands?"

Instead of a response, Xil pressed both his hands on the table, palms down. A strange light pulsed from underneath, then the metal surface began to boil. I blinked, trying to understand what was going on. A second later, a perfectly formed set of utensils lay next to Xil's hands. Not quite a knife and fork like we would have used on Earth, but quite similar.

"They're custom created for each guest," he explained. "You can take yours home with you after as a souvenir. Look, it's even got the restaurant's logo embossed."

I copied him, and to my relief, the metal didn't actually boil. The temperature stayed the same and within an instant, I had a fork and spoon. No knife. Finally looking at my food, I understood that I wouldn't need one. It was a sort of stew with green and blue bits floating in a dark liquid. And it was smoking. Not steaming like any sizzling dish would, but smoking as if it had just been on fire. I sneezed.

"That would be the burnt yaki roots," Havel said, already digging into his own meal which was smoking in the same way. "They don't taste like much raw or even boiled, but if you burn them, they release their flavour. Only the best cooks know how to infuse a dish with yaki root smoke. I've only had it once or twice before."

Okay then. This evening was becoming weirder and weirder. My food had been seasoned with smoke and tiny metal fragments. Normal. Totally normal.

My stomach growled, and I decided it was time to push all my questions aside. While the stew didn't look as appetising as I'd hoped, it smelled delicious.

And it tasted divine. My tongue may have had an orgasm after I swallowed the first spoonful.

Flavours exploded in my mouth, so full of depth

that I was sure I'd never tasted anything this amazing before. Layers upon layers of taste overwhelmed my senses, but not too much so that I couldn't wolf down the stew.

We ate in silence, all of us completely occupied with our food. I even forgot that I'd wanted to try the guys' dishes. By the time I'd emptied my bowl, I was stuffed to the top and wouldn't have been able to even squeeze in a single scoop of ice cream. Which was almost unheard of. 'There's always space for ice cream because it melts and runs into all the little gaps', my grandma used to say. Alien stew had proven her wrong for the very first time.

I leaned back, sated and a little sleepy.

"Would anyone like dessert?" the waiter suddenly asked. I was in such a food coma that I hadn't even noticed them approach.

"No," we said as one.

Havel groaned a little. He had three empty bowls in front of him - no idea how he'd managed to eat all that.

"Do you require a private space to ruminate?" they asked.

I stared at them. "Ruminate? Like a cow?"

"Some species do that," Matar whispered. "Others will expel the food they've just eaten just so they can try more of the dishes on offer."

Like in Ancient Rome. Disgusting. And such a waste of food.

"Just the bill, please," Xil said with a wry smile. "And could you order us a shuttle?"

A strange pain suddenly erupted in my stomach, like I was being stabbed from within. I clutched my belly but tried not to let the guys notice.

"Where's the loo?" I asked the waiter and got to my feet.

"Follow me," they said, but as soon as I'd taken the first step, the pain exploded into agony and I collapsed to the floor, unable to even break my fall.

"Trish!"

"What's wrong?"

The pain was making it hard to breathe, hard to think. Blackness teetered at the edges of my vision as I curled into a ball, praying that this would be over soon.

LESSON 9

FIRST AID FOR PANICKED MALES

XIL

My mate was writhing in agony. Her face was deathly pale, the only colour her red-rimmed eyes. Tears ran down her cheeks as she screamed in pain.

"I'm not feeling too well," Havel suddenly groaned and then he went down, too. Klat, he was our medic, the male supposed to help Trish. Now he was on the floor, clutching his belly, clearly unable to help anyone, least of all himself.

"I'll get help," the waiter shouted and ran off.

I kneeled by Trish's side while Matar checked on Havel.

"It's going to be alright, love," I whispered and lay my hand on her hot forehead. She was burning up. "Help is coming. You'll be back to normal in no time. Just hold on, little human, hold on."

I didn't know what to say or do. I was helpless. It was the worst feeling in the universe. Trish was in pain, and there was no way I could make her better. If I could have taken her pain, I would have without hesitation. I was prepared to feel the burning whip of the Great A'Ta on my back if it meant Trish wasn't suffering. And I didn't even believe in A'Ta.

"He's running a fever," Matar reported. "His fangs are extended. Not sure what that means."

Trish didn't have fangs I could check to see if it was a shared symptom.

It took the waiter an eternity to return with four other beings, two of them wearing the same loincloth while the others' white suits identified them as medics.

"What happened?" one of the healers asked and pushed me aside. She was a petite Ankani, but the authority in her voice made me obey her immediately.

"She just collapsed, holding her stomach. A few minutes later, my friend did the same. They're both in agony. You'll have to give them something for the pain."

"I'll decide what to give them," she snapped. "Did they eat the same food?"

"No. She had a vegetable and root stew while he had a loomani sausage. You'll have to ask the waiter if any of the ingredients were the same."

"Yaki roots!" Matar exclaimed before the waiter had the chance to speak. "They both had yaki root smoke infused with their meals."

Klat. He was right. I'd never heard of yaki root being poisonous, but it wasn't my area of expertise.

"Peti'i, get me the antidote," the medic ordered the other healer while at the same time rummaging in her bag. She pulled out two syringes, stabbed one of them in Trish's upper arm, and then hurried over to Havel to give him the same injection. "That's going to stabilise them until we've got the antidote. Yaki root can be poisonous when burned for too short a period, but I wouldn't have expected this to happen in this restaurant."

"I'll... I'll tell the cook," the waiter stammered and ran off.

"Get the manager, too!" I shouted after him. "I've got a thing or two to say to them."

Fury raced through my veins, and I had a hard time not to attack the remaining two waiters standing in the background. This was a clear case of negligence. They could have killed my mate and my friend.

I growled.

"Xil?"

Trish opened her eyes and looked right at me. Some of the anger dissipated into relief.

"Are you still in pain?" I asked and stroked her forehead again.

"Of course she is," the medic admonished me. "Don't ask such stupid questions. I've given her some light pain killers, but I can't give them anything stronger until we have the antidote. The two drugs might interact, and I don't want to risk that."

"Hold my hand?" Trish asked weakly, and I was only too willing to oblige. She barely had to strength to return my grip on her hand. It scared me.

I looked over at Havel. He was no longer writhing in pain either, but his face was pale and his fangs were still extended. He tried to hide his pain, just like Trish, but it was clear that both of them were suffering. I was going to kill that cook. We'd come here to have a wonderful evening, to celebrate our completed nest. This was a disaster.

The other medic returned, holding a metal lockbox. I squeezed Trish's hand. "Not much longer now, little human. You're going to be fine."

"You might want to step back," the female medic warned me. "The antidote might induce vomiting, and you don't want to be in the line of fire."

I didn't move. "I don't mind. My mate needs me."

Matar didn't leave Havel's side either. I was proud of my friends, my family. We stood together even in the face of adversity and vomit.

Luckily, it never came to that. As soon as the medic had injected Trish and Havel with the antidote, colour returned to their faces.

"Wow, that worked fast," Trish said and sat up without needing help. I wrapped an arm around her shoulders to steady her, just in case - plus after almost losing her, I needed the physical contact. It took all my mental strength not to throw her over my shoulder, carry her to our ship and ravish her in the nest until we'd both forgotten about today's events.

"No nausea?" the medic asked but was interrupted by loud retching from Havel. One of the waiters handed him a bowl and my poor friend started filling it with the contents of his stomach.

The healer looked almost pleased. "Just like I said, the drug can cause vomiting. You'll both be fine. Don't eat anything today, but drink lots of fluids. Go to bed early and rest. Tomorrow you should be able to eat normally again, but maybe avoid yaki roots for a while."

"Never again," I growled.

I helped Trish to her feet but kept my arms around her. I wasn't going to let go of her any time soon.

"I'm fine," she muttered, but she didn't try to get out

of my embrace. On the contrary, she leaned against my chest, just the way I liked it.

The waiter arrived with three other aliens in tow. The largest of them, a species I'd not encountered before, wore an apron covered with stains. The cook, I presumed. The other two were clad in business suits, a female with a bright green mane and a fellow Kardarian male.

He greeted me with the traditional fist-on-chest gesture, but I didn't return it. I wanted to greet him with fist-on-nose and fist-to-his-balls, but luckily I had my arms around Trish and attacking him would have meant letting go of her.

"I apologise on behalf of the entire Outer Ring Restaurant," the male said. "I can't explain how this happened. We've never had any issues like this before, but of course, our cook will be disciplined."

The flabby cook had the decency to look guilty. Maybe the punishment should be him ingesting poisonous yaki roots. That way he could feel the pain he'd inflicted on my family.

"We will, of course, compensate you for your troubles," the Kardarian continued. "We have a new restaurant that just opened on Labeari, the resort planet near the Kepler Two space station. How about two weeks all-inclusive at the resort with all expenses paid? Plus a generous stipend so you can enjoy all the pleasures Labeari has to offer?"

"Are you trying to bribe us?" I snarled. "I assume in

return you don't want us to tell anyone about the poisonous yaki?"

The male took a step back, fear flashing across his face before he smoothed his expression. "Not at all. I just want to make sure you all have a relaxing time to recover from what happened. How about we throw in money for fuel and some delicacies to sustain you during your journey? Plus any salary you might miss out on during your holiday?"

"We'll take it," Trish said before I could attack the slimy Kardarian. He was a shame to our species, weaselling his way out of the situation. "But we want three weeks plus free food at all your restaurants for a whole year."

The male's eyes widened just a fraction before he nodded. "Agreed. And you won't tell the media about this, right?"

"Our ship could use an upgrade to our engine," Matar said from behind me. "We'd want to travel to Labeari as fast as possible."

"Obviously." The Kardarian sighed. "I'll make the necessary arrangements. Again, I apologise for the inconvenience."

He walked off, followed by everyone except the original waiter.

"I'm so sorry," they said, before also shuffling away.

Havel's laugh interrupted the moment of silence that echoed their departure. "We got a good deal. Might have been worth the pain." I turned just in time to see him bend over his bowl again.

Poor guy.

Professor Katila looked angrier than I'd ever seen before. I hadn't thought Karangi could get this furious. They were known for being benevolent, kind and intelligent, but right now, Katila didn't seem any of those. Her middle eye was blazing with anger as she stared us down through the video link.

"Say that again," she hissed.

"We quit," I said calmly for the third time in a row. "We'll no longer be part of your course. We don't care what grade you give us for the beginners' class. We don't care at all about you and the IGU. All we want is to be left in peace and spend time with our mate."

"You would never have found your mate without my course. I never expected you to be such ungrateful-"

"Ungrateful?" I repeated. "You basically blackmailed us into becoming part of your case study. You should be grateful that we agreed to that. And you've only got yourself to blame. If you hadn't kidnapped Trish, we might still be willing to cooperate with you."

"I didn't kidnap her," Katila seethed. "I only commissioned it."

"How is that any different," Trish demanded furiously. "Just because you didn't get your hands dirty doesn't mean you're innocent. Just accept it, we're quitting. We've got better things to do than dance to your tune."

"You'll regret this. All the time and resources I invested in you... you're going to pay for it. I will have to start my research from scratch. So many hours wasted... You better watch your back. Yaki roots aren't the only poisonous things out there."

She ended the transmission before I could reply. I turned to the others. Their shock mirrored my own.

"How did she know?" Havel asked. "We didn't tell anyone about the yaki. Do you think that was her doing, too?"

"I wouldn't put it past her," Trish said. "She doesn't seem to respect laws and ethics, so what would stop her from bribing the cook to poison us?"

"But to what end?" I questioned. "What good would that do? The kidnapping was a test to see how we'd react and if we'd manage to rescue you. As awful as it was, you were never in real danger. If we'd not saved you, they would have released you eventually. Poisoning you and Havel is an entirely different matter. You could have died. Why would Katila want that?"

"If I was gone, she could have made you abduct more humans. That's what she wanted from the start. It would have fit her course. It's called Alien Abduction for Beginners, after all, not Alien Mating With The Female You Abducted."

"I don't know. As much as I loathe her, I don't think she'd go that far. She's watching us, who knows, maybe she had a spy in that restaurant?"

Havel sighed. "It doesn't matter. We're free of her now, that's what counts. As much as I wanted to have that certificate to show our families that we're proper abductors, it's not worth the trouble."

Trish nodded. "It's the knowledge that counts, not the qualification. You know how abductions work - not that I'll ever let you abduct another female." She laughed. "I'm the only abductee in your life and that's what it'll stay like."

Matar pulled her onto his lap. "Yes. It's perfect. You, us, the Jade. And your little tribitt."

Her pet was sleeping in a basket by her feet. While the animal loved cuddles while it was awake, it preferred to sleep without being touched. It had actually growled at me earlier when I'd got too close to the basket. He had slept through our launch from the space station. I was glad he hadn't got scared, but we had yet to see how he would react when we encountered some space turbulence.

"That reminds me, he needs a name," Trish said. "And I don't want to decide that myself. I want it to be something meaningful for all of us."

"Is this what it's going to be like once we have offspring?" I asked with genuine curiosity.

"No offspring any time soon. But once we do get pregnant, then yes, I'd like us all to come up with names together."

"*We* get pregnant?" Havel repeated. "I'm sorry to disappoint you, but Kardarian males don't have a uterus."

Trish laughed until tears appeared in her pretty eyes. "It's just an expression. I'm going to be the one carrying our baby, but it's something you will all be involved in."

"Of course. We'll watch over you every minute of the day," I told her. "We'll massage your feet, we'll cook your meals, we'll hold your boobs when they get too heavy."

Trish broke into laughter again. Her cheeks were bright red, and I was starting to get worried. "Uhm... no boob holding required. I've got a bra for that. Although... I won't say no to you doing that while we're in our nest."

"My hands are much warmer than your silly bras. I'm sure you'll change your mind once your breasts are full of milk for our hungry offspring. I remember my aunt sitting on my uncle's lap all day, him holding her breasts..."

I stopped because she was still laughing.

Havel looked at his communicator. "Careful, chicken, you're not getting enough oxygen."

That made her laugh even harder. Had we broken our human?

"What names were you thinking of?" I asked to distract her. I didn't want her to suffocate.

"Maybe something to do with his colour," she said, her voice now hoarse from all the laughing. "What's the Kardarian word for green?"

"Skweke," Havel replied.

"No, that's too hard to pronounce. We need

something cuter. On Earth, we have a green plant that's considered lucky. Clover. Is there a translation for that?"

I shook my head. "Not that I know of. We don't have many green plants on Kardar."

She looked at me as if I was crazy. "Your plants aren't green? What about the grass?"

"Grass is a Peritus thing. Our planet's surface is covered in fur."

I didn't think her eyes could get any wider. "Fur? Like animal fur? You're kidding me, right?"

"No, not animal fur. Plant fur. It might be that your translator doesn't have an equivalent word for it. But anyway, we don't have that... clover."

The little tribitt raised his head as if he knew that we were talking about him. He squeaked, an adorable sound that immediately made me want to pick him up and cuddle him. I bet that was a trait designed by the pet breeders.

"So cute," Trish cooed. "How about squeak?"

"The translation for that would be boop," Matar said. "Not boob, like your beautiful boobs. Boop."

"Boop," our mate repeated as if tasting the word. "Boop. I like it. Boobieboop. Boopboop. Booooooop."

"We've broken her," I whispered to the others. "Maybe it's an aftereffect of the poison?"

"Boop it is," Trish announced. "Lord Boop, since he's the first of all the pets we're going to have."

I exchanged a look with Havel and Matar. Giving her the tribitt had been a massive mistake.

TRISH

I was getting used to the nest. Lying on the exploding-colour-sheet with pillows surrounding me from all sides made me feel both comfortable and safe. Plus the three naked guys were a definite bonus. Havel was to my right, Matar to my left and I was spread across Xil. We'd ignored the doctor's advice to take it easy. I bet she wouldn't have been able to resist these males either.

It felt right. Our bodies touched, turning us into one being. We were not longer four separate people. In this nest, we were one.

"I never thought I could feel this happy," I whispered. "How is this even possible?"

"Only A'Ta knows," Matar replied solemnly. "He has led us together and blessed our mating."

"Or maybe it was destiny, not some deity's doing," Havel said, but there was no animosity in his tone. We both accepted Matar's beliefs, even though we didn't share them.

"However we got together, I'm never letting you go," I told them. "You're mine until the end of the universe."

"And you are ours," Xil whispered and kissed the nape of my neck. His hot breath made my skin tingle and heat spread through my body, pooling between my legs. As if I hadn't just fucked all three of them. We should probably sleep like that medic had recommended. I felt fine, but I wasn't sure about Havel. He'd been more affected by the antidote than I had. The poor guy.

I reached out to him and stroked his hard chest. The greenish freckles on his otherwise blue skin seemed to move beneath my touch. If I hadn't been so comfortable on top of Xil, I would have climbed on Havel and licked those spots. He loved that.

Matar's tail twitched where it was wrapped around my thigh, and I chuckled, starting to stroke his chest as well. He purred and grasped my hand, leading it down until my fingers touched his cock. He was hard again, rock hard and ready to plunge into my depths. Maybe sleep could wait...

Suddenly, all the lights in the room started flashing, and an ear-shattering siren made me sit up straight.

"What's happening?" I screamed against the noise.

The guys jumped up, and Xil pulled me to my feet. He grabbed my shoulders, his eyes wild with emotion.

"We're under attack!"

The siren stopped, and a very familiar voice echoed through the room.

"I decided not to wait. It's time for you to hand over the human." Professor Katila sounded genuinely deranged. "I'll let you live if you do. You'll go back to working for me. If not..."

The Jade lurched to one side, and I would have fallen if Xil hadn't caught me just in time.

"You're all going to die."

The story continues in Alien Abduction for Experts.

If you haven't already taken your Intergalactic University exam, flick the page to take the test.

Want more books? Subscribe to my newsletter: skyemackinnon.com/newsletter

PIKI CAKES RECIPE

For the first time ever, the Intaran Bakers' Association has given permission for a version of their famous piki cake recipe to be printed. Of course, some (or all) ingredients had to be replaced with Peritan equivalents. Actually, these might be nothing like the real piki cakes that the whole galaxy raves about, but it'll give you a general idea. Or not.

Bake at your own peril.

But seriously, they're delicious.

INGREDIENTS

- 50g butter at room temperature (or softened if you live in a cold place like space)
- ¼ cup brown sugar
- 50g plain yogurt

- 1 egg
- 1 cup self-raising flour
- ½ cup rye flour (or brown flour)
- 100g dark chocolate, chopped, or chocolate chips
- 1 ½ tablespoons cacao powder
- 1 cup cooked beetroot – about 140 grams

INSTRUCTIONS

1. Preheat the oven to 170C/340F, line a baking tray.
2. Grate or puree the beetroot.
3. Beat the butter, sugar and yogurt in a bowl until well combined. Add the egg.
4. Stir in the remaining ingredients, adding the beetroot last.
5. Shape the biscuits into small balls and place on the baking tray. If the dough is too moist, add some more flour.
6. Flatten the biscuits with the back of a spoon or your fingers.
7. Bake for 12-14 minutes.
8. Cool on a tray.
9. If desired, sprinkle with icing sugar or cocoa.
10. Devour.

COULD YOU ABDUCT A HUMAN?

Do you think you've got what it takes to become an alien abductor? Take this test to find out!
skyemackinnon.com/alien-abduction-test

(if you share your results on social media, be sure to tag me)

And if you feel like you've passed this course, you can download a certificate!
hi.switchy.io/AAFBcertificate

THE INTERGALACTIC GUIDE TO HUMANS

Abductions aren't easy - which is exactly why the Intergalactic University offers a range of courses at various levels. Immerse yourself in this strange, comical universe and work on your abduction skills.

Find all books in this series here:

skyemackinnon.com/intergalactic-guide

Alien Abduction for Beginners

Alien Abduction for Professionals

Alien Abduction for Experts

(reverse harem/why choose trilogy, to be read in order)

Alien Abduction for Santa

(fmf standalone)

Alien Abduction for Pirates

(mf standalone)

Alien Abduction for Milkmen

(mm standalone)

Alien Abduction for Unicorns

(mf standalone)

THE STARLIGHT UNIVERSE

This book is part of the Starlight Universe, an entire galaxy filled with hunky aliens, exotic planets, and the human women ready to find love among the stars.

Starlight Highlanders Mail Order Brides

Alien Highlanders in kilts come to Earth in search of brides... and take them to planet Albya. Three m/f standalones full of humour, action and steamy romance. Part of the Intergalactic Dating Agency.

The Intergalactic Guide to Humans

A humorous take on alien abductions, probing and other shenanigans. One reverse harem trilogy about clueless aliens and the human woman they abducted, followed by several standalone romances with various pairings (m/f, f/m/f and m/m). If you want light entertainment filled with unicorns, fabulous misunderstandings and unusual body parts, this is the series for you.

Starlight Vikings

Set on Earth and on the spaceship Valkyr, this trilogy of m/f standalones is all about hunky alien Vikings in need of females. Part of the Intergalactic Dating Agency.

Starlight Monsters

These aliens are not your usual humanoids... they have claws, fangs, tails, scales, knotty dicks and will growl at you. Interconnected m/f standalones with lots of action, steam and fated mates.

ABOUT THE AUTHOR

Skye MacKinnon is a Scottish romance author who was raised by elves in the mystical Highlands and calls the Loch Ness monster her friend. Her bestselling books weave together romance with action, suspense and whimsical humour, creating page-turners filled with strong heroines, alpha heroes and loveable monsters.

Whether she's writing about aliens in kilts, hunky Vikings or cat shifter assassins, Skye likes to put a new spin on familiar tropes. Some of her heroines don't have to choose, some fall in love with other women, and others get abducted by clueless aliens.

Skye lives with her bossy cat on the west coast of Scotland and uses the dramatic views from her office as an inspiration, no matter whether she writes fantasy, paranormal or science fiction romance. Until she gets abducted by aliens, that is.

Subscribe to her newsletter:

skyemackinnon.com/newsletter

ALSO BY SKYE MACKINNON

Find all of Skye's books on her website, skyemackinnon.com, where you can also order signed paperbacks and swag. Many of her books are available as audiobooks.

PARANORMAL & FANTASY ROMANCE

- **Claiming Her Bears** (post-apocalyptic shifter reverse harem)
- **Daughter of Winter** (fantasy reverse harem)
- **Catnip Assassins** (urban fantasy reverse harem)
- **Infernal Descent** (paranormal reverse harem based on Dante's Inferno, co-written with Bea Paige)
- **Seven Wardens** (fantasy reverse harem co-written with Laura Greenwood)
- **The Lost Siren** (post-apocalyptic, paranormal reverse harem co-written with Liza Street)

SCIENCE FICTION ROMANCE

- **Starlight Highlanders Mail Order Brides** (sci-fi m/f romance, part of the Intergalactic Dating Agency)
- **Starlight Vikings** (sci-fi m/f romance, part of the Intergalactic Dating Agency)
- **Starlight Monsters** (m/f romance)
- **The Intergalactic Guide to Humans** (sci-fi romance with various pairings)
- **Between Rebels** (sci-fi reverse harem set in the Planet Athion shared world)
- **The Mars Diaries** (sci-fi reverse harem)
- **Through the Gates** (dystopian reverse harem co-written with Rebecca Royce)
- **Aliens and Animals** (f/f sci-fi romance co-written with Arizona Tape)

OTHER SERIES

- **Academy of Time** (time travel academy standalones, reverse harem and m/f)
- **Defiance** (contemporary reverse harem with a hint of thriller/suspense)

STANDALONES

- Song of Souls – m/f fantasy romance, fairy tale retelling
- Wings of Time and Fate - YA fantasy

- Their Hybrid – steampunk reverse harem
- Partridge in the P.E.A.R. - sci-fi reverse harem co-written with Arizona Tape
- Highland Butterflies – lesbian romance

BOX SETS

- Daggers & Destiny – a Skye MacKinnon starter library
- Stars & Seduction - a Sci-Fi Romance starter library

www.ingramcontent.com/pod-product-compliance
Ingram Content Group UK Ltd.
Pitfield, Milton Keynes, MK11 3LW, UK
UKHW040008200726
13854UKWH00001B/104

9 798201 473938